Melissa gazed up at him. Her eyes darkened, her gaze fluttering down to settle on his mouth.

His breath hitched, trapped somewhere deep in his lungs. He bent toward her, his own gaze fixed on the Cupid's bow curve of her pink lips.

He wanted to taste her. He wanted it more than he wanted his next breath.

In the distance, a dog barked. She stepped away from him.

Aching with frustration, he followed her up the sidewalk to the house. As they neared the wooden porch steps, something just in front of the first step glittered in the morning sunlight, catching Aaron's eye.

His heart jumped into his throat. "Stop!"

Melissa jerked to a halt.

"That," he said, "is a trip wire."

"What?"

"Melissa, I think there's a bomb somewhere around your porch."

PAULA GRAVES

BACHELOR SHERIFF

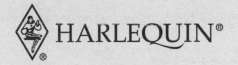

TORONTO • NEW YORK • LONDON
AMSTERDAM • PARIS • SYDNEY • HAMBURG
STOCKHOLM • ATHENS • TOKYO • MILAN • MADRID
PRAGUE • WARSAW • BUDAPEST • AUCKLAND

For Jenn, who makes me a better writer every time.

Recycling programs
for this product may
not exist in your area.

ISBN-13: 978-0-373-69497-6

BACHELOR SHERIFF

Copyright © 2010 by Paula Graves

ABOUT THE AUTHOR

Alabama native Paula Graves wrote her first book, a mystery starring herself and her neighborhood friends, at the age of six. A voracious reader, Paula loves books that pair tantalizing mystery with compelling romance. When she's not reading or writing, she works as a creative director for a Birmingham advertising agency and spends time with her family and friends. She is a member of Southern Magic Romance Writers, Heart of Dixie Romance Writers and Romance Writers of America.

Paula invites readers to visit her Web site, www.paulagraves.com.

Books by Paula Graves

CAST OF CHARACTERS

Melissa Draper—This contracts lawyer knows she's not the type of woman who inspires passion, good or bad. So why is someone going to dangerous lengths to see her dead?

Aaron Cooper—Melissa's high school crush has grown up to be a well-known heartbreaker. He's also the deputy sheriff assigned to investigate her case.

Riley Patterson—Aaron's brother-in-law proves to be invaluable help investigating the attempts on Melissa's life. But is he also right about Aaron's growing feelings for Melissa?

Derek Draper—Melissa's father is well-known around town as an upstanding citizen. But Melissa knows he has a dark side.

Carter Morgan—Melissa's boss is also her trusted mentor.

Alice Gaines—Melissa's coworker is on vacation, but is it odd that nobody can reach her at all?

Dalton Brant—Melissa's fellow lawyer is jealous of her relationship with their boss, Carter Morgan. Is he jealous enough to want her out of the picture altogether?

Amy DeLong—When Melissa's friend becomes the victim of an attack meant for Melissa, the attempted murder could give them a clue about the killer's identity.

Evan Hallman—Melissa's ex-boyfriend has a very good motive for revenge against Melissa, but he's safely locked away in another state. Or is he?

Chapter One

Jasper's low whine jarred Melissa Draper awake. Blinking to clear the sleep from her eyes, she peered into the inky gloom at the foot of her bed, where the Beagle-mix puppy usually slept. But Jasper wasn't there.

Her heart quickening, she sat upright. "Jasper?"

She kicked off the bedcovers and shivered, surprised to find the room had grown frigidly cold during the night. From the doorway, Jasper whimpered softly.

Melissa turned on the bedside lamp. Nothing happened. The digital alarm clock on her bedside table was also dark.

The power must be out. That explained the cold.

Outages weren't unusual where Melissa lived. Fallen tree limbs, lightning strikes—any number of events could cause a break in her power supply. She'd bought a gasoline generator last year for that very reason.

She kept a flashlight in the bedside table drawer. She found it and turned it on. A beam of light sliced the darkness, bouncing off a light haze.

Then the acrid smell of smoke hit her nose.

"Come, Jasper." She grabbed her robe and entered the narrow hallway. The puppy kept pace as she headed for the stairs.

As the smell of burning wood and plastic assaulted her in

a bitter cloud, her heart rate soared. Now she could hear the faint shriek of the smoke detector going off downstairs.

Her house was on fire.

The hallway smoke detector went off right over her head, making her jump. Leaning against the wall, her hand over her galloping heart, she tried to think what to do next.

The phone in her room depended on electricity, but her cell phone usually worked, even this far out of town. It was in her purse downstairs. She had to get to it.

Gagging on the acrid haze, she crouched low and hurried to the top of the stairs. She paused there, peering down the steep stairs, her head swimming. She hated heights, even in full daylight when she could see each step down. With the bottom floor barely visible through the smoky haze, the dizzy sensation was that much worse.

Clinging to the rail all the way down, she reached the first floor unscathed. The smoke seemed to be coming from the back of the house, near the kitchen. Had she left the stove on?

She dropped to her knees, crawling through the thickening smoke toward her purse on the foyer table. Purse in hand, she groped her way to the door, reached up and twisted the dead bolt.

Nothing happened.

She tugged at the dead bolt again, but the lock didn't turn.

Beside her Jasper started to bark wildly, startling her. "It's okay, buddy, we're going to be okay." She could get out through the windows, breaking one if it didn't open.

First, she had to stay calm and think, while she still had time. What could she save before the fire consumed it?

Her pro bono files were in a metal file cabinet down the hall, but there were copies of those on disks in a safe-deposit box at the bank, plus digital copies of vital records on her laptop as well. The work files in the cabinet were just copies of files stored at the law office. There were some photos she didn't want to lose, but she wouldn't risk her life going back upstairs for them. Clothes, food and appliances could be replaced by the insurance check. All she had to save were her purse, her notebook computer and her dog.

She swung the long strap of her purse over her neck and grabbed the attaché case containing her notebook computer. "Let's go, Jasper."

Out of the corner of her eye, she spotted movement outside. Turning her head, she saw what might have been a shadowy figure disappear past the far window facing the front porch.

She froze for a second, until a popping sound coming from the kitchen spurred her into action again. She dug her phone from her purse and dialed 911, reaching out to calm her frantic dog. "Jasper, shh…"

A female voice answered. "Chickasaw County 911."

"This is Melissa Draper. I live on Tuckahaw Road, south of the bridge. My house is on fire." Reaching up, she tried the door again. The lock wouldn't budge. "I'm also having trouble getting out of the house."

After a brief pause, the woman replied, "We've got units on the way. Is there a first floor window you can open?"

Melissa peered up at the windows that looked out on the porch. The memory of the mysterious shadow gave her a moment's pause. Had someone set the fire deliberately? Maybe cut the power to the house?

Was he outside, waiting for her?

She'd have to take the risk.

She pushed to her feet. "I'm putting the phone in the pocket of my robe. Just a minute." She swept the window drapes aside. Moonlight washed the front porch outside with cold blue light, dimmed by a light haze from the fire at the back of her house. From her vantage point, she saw nothing and no one moving outside.

She unlocked the window and tugged at the sash. Decades of old paint put up a fight, but she finally heard a soft crack over the wail of the smoke alarm, and the window rattled open. She unlatched the screen and pushed it onto the porch. It fell with a soft clatter.

"Come on, Jasper." She picked up the trembling dog and lowered him out the window onto the porch. Pulling up the hem of her robe, she crawled out the window in a hurry, hauling her purse and attaché over the sill with her. She landed with an awkward thump on the porch beside her frantic, barking puppy.

"We're out," she said into her cell phone, her gaze sweeping the front lawn for any sign of intruders. All she saw was winter-browned grass spreading twenty yards square, hemmed by woods on both sides and the narrow lane in front.

"You need to get away from the house. Head to a neighbor's house if it's too cold to wait outside," the 911 operator suggested.

Melissa's Volkswagen GTI sat in the driveway, a safe distance from the house. She and Jasper could wait there.

On her way to the porch steps, she paused by the door. Shining her flashlight on the dead bolt, she caught her breath when she spotted a small stick wedged into the keyhole. That's why she hadn't been able to unlock the front door.

Had someone put the stick there on purpose?

In the distance, wailing sirens broke the silence of the dark night. Melissa kept moving, clicking her fingers at Jasper and hoping he was unnerved enough by their current ordeal to follow her rather than haring off in all directions the way he usually did when he was off his leash. To her relief, he stayed close, hopping right into the car when she opened the door.

The car's interior was frigidly cold, making her wish that she'd considered her warm winter coat one of the necessary things to save from the fire. She doubted the cold engine would generate enough heat to make a difference before the firemen arrived, so she didn't risk it, huddling close to Jasper, grateful, for once, to have his warm puppy breath in her face.

A column of thick black smoke roiled from the back of her house. No flames visible yet, but a faint glow tinted the rising smoke and she tried not to think too hard about what parts of her house might be burning to the ground while she waited for the firemen to arrive.

She checked the car door locks one more time. Someone had stuck that twig in the dead bolt. Might have been a prank, but what if it wasn't? If Jasper hadn't started whining when he did, she might not have awakened until fire had engulfed the entire house. The time wasted trying to open the sabotaged door could have been the difference between living and dying.

But who would have done such a thing?

"ARSON?" Aaron Cooper blinked sluggishly at his alarm clock. 4:35 a.m. He pushed himself to a sitting position on the side of the bed and listened to the Chickasaw County Sheriff's Department dispatcher rattle off the address over the phone. "Okay, on my way."

He dressed quickly and snapped his service pistol, a lethal black Smith & Wesson M&P40, into his lightweight belt holster, unable to hold back a smile as he did so. His recent promotion to the Sheriff's Department Investigative Unit had a few perks, he had to admit. Like losing the bulky duty belt that came with the patrol uniform.

The January predawn was as cold as it had looked through his bedroom window. He tugged his leather jacket more tightly around him and headed for the Ford F-10 parked in his driveway.

All Dispatch had told him was that a complainant had called in a suspicious fire to 911. Apparently no casualties, thank God, but if someone had tried to burn the house down around the owner it was attempted murder and a pretty damned big deal, especially in a quiet rural place like Chickasaw County.

He left the Gossamer Ridge city limits and headed southeast toward the county line. The address was Tuckahaw Road, which he knew from his days on patrol was mostly woods dotted with the occasional farm. Once he crossed the old steel bridge that spanned the meandering waters of Tuckahaw Branch, the houses were fewer and farther between along the twisting country road.

After another sharp curve, the road straightened, and Aaron spotted a fire engine and two Chickasaw County Sheriff's Department cruisers parked haphazardly in front of a two-story farmhouse ahead. The house was still standing, he noted as he pulled his truck behind the closest cruiser. That was a plus.

One of his fellow deputies, Blake Clayton, greeted him as he approached. "Fire made a mess of the kitchen area, but the truck got here in time to stop it from spreading."

"Started in the kitchen?" Aaron fell into step with Blake as the deputy led him to the back of the house. A kitchen fire didn't sound much like arson.

"Back of the house behind the kitchen, actually," Blake corrected. Rounding the corner, they found a couple of firefighters, still clad in their heavy slickers and rubber boots, crouched in front of the charred remains of what looked to be a gas generator.

One of the firemen moved, revealing a small, slim woman standing a few feet behind him, a frown creasing her forehead as she watched the firemen investigating the scorched areas behind the house. Homeowner, Aaron guessed. She looked familiar.

Her gaze shifted, bumping with his. Her mouth fell open slightly, her blue eyes widening with a flicker of recognition. He searched his brain for where he knew her. Definitely not an ex-girlfriend; he'd never gone for brunettes, although he had to admit he was intrigued by this particular brunette, even as disheveled and smoke-smudged as she was at the moment. She dropped her gaze, and he felt an odd sense of disappointment.

Blake Clayton spoke to the woman. "Ms. Draper? This is Deputy Cooper, one of the Sheriff's Department investigators. Deputy Cooper, this is Melissa Draper, the homeowner."

Memories clicked into place. Melissa Draper. From his high school graduating class. Geeky, shy, total brainiac. No wonder he hadn't remembered her at first. He'd have barely remembered her back in high school.

Not that he was particularly proud of that fact.

Aaron held out his hand for a shake, then dropped it as he realized Melissa's arms were wrapped around a shivering puppy. The dog looked up at him with scared brown eyes and let out a soft moan somewhere between a whimper and a howl.

"Deputy Cooper and I have met," Melissa said to Blake, though her gaze remained locked with Aaron's. He felt an odd flutter in the center of his chest. "I thought you'd be off playing pro football somewhere."

He felt an old, bitter twinge of regret. "Blew out my knee first week of training camp, so I had to find another career."

She looked genuinely sympathetic. He wouldn't have blamed her for indulging in a little pleasure at his downfall instead. High school social politics had been brutal, and people like Melissa Draper had always ended up outside the in-crowd.

"What about you? What're you doing these days?" he asked.

"I'm a lawyer." She didn't bother to hide the touch of pride in her voice.

Figured. She'd been voted most likely to succeed, hadn't she? Something like that.

The puppy whined again, drawing Aaron's attention back to the present. The poor thing was shivering. Melissa didn't look much warmer herself. Time to get his mind back on the job and get the two of them someplace warm and safe.

He addressed the two firemen who'd continued examining the charred generator while he'd been talking to Melissa. "Any verdict yet, guys?"

Perry Davis, the younger of the two and an old high school teammate, glanced at Aaron. "Still looking."

"How much longer before I can have my house back?" Melissa asked quietly. She was stroking the puppy's head soothingly, shushing his occasional whimpers, and looked ready to pass out from stress and exhaustion.

"The damage is limited to your kitchen, but the power company's gonna have to reroute your power supply. You don't have a generator anymore, and even if you did, it would still require pretty massive rewiring before you'd get any juice to your house." Perry Davis gave her an apologetic look. "I figure it'll be at least a week. Depends on how quickly the power company can get technicians on the scene and whether your insurance company will want a further investigation first."

Melissa looked ready to crumple into a heap right at Aaron's feet. He reached out, cupping her elbow. She gave a start, pulling away to look at him with wary eyes.

He dropped his hand away, guilty about giving her a fright.

Her nerves were probably stretched to the snapping point at the moment. "You can probably call your insurance agent as early as seven," he murmured, gesturing for her to follow him away from the damage site. "Meanwhile, let's get you and Scooter here somewhere warm."

Her lips twitched at his words. "His name is Jasper," she corrected softly. "And somewhere warm sounds wonderful."

"I'll drive you to your folks' place. They're still out on Hickory Bluff Road, right?"

"No," she said quickly, darting him a look of dismay that caught him by surprise. "I mean, yes, they still live on Hickory Bluff Road, but I don't want to go there. I can find a hotel near my office—"

"Hotels won't take Jasper." A sudden image flashed through his mind, catching him off guard— a picture of himself taking Melissa home to his own house, filling her full of hot chocolate and tucking her and her whiny puppy beneath the warm covers of his bed. Ruthlessly, he pushed the surprising image aside.

"I'll find somewhere to stay," she insisted, although he could see the wheels of her mind churning desperately for a solution to her problem.

"You could stay at my folks' place. They have a guest cottage they keep up for situations just like this."

She arched a dark eyebrow at him. "They take in a lot of house fire refugees?"

"Okay, maybe not situations *exactly* like this."

"There's still the problem of Jasper," she said.

"Is he house-trained?"

"Yes, but—"

"Not a problem." He glanced at his watch. It was after five o'clock now. His parents were early risers. "I'll give Mom a call, set it up." He turned to Blake, who was looking at him with a puzzled expression. "What?"

"Nothing," Blake said, but the puzzled look didn't go away.

"Perry, is Ms. Draper okay to go upstairs and pack a bag for herself?"

Perry looked away from his examination of the ground around the ruined generator. "Oh, yeah. The damage inside was limited to the kitchen, and the structural supports look like they avoided any major damage."

Aaron put his hand on Melissa's shoulder. She flinched again, and he dropped his hand away. "Sorry."

"You just startled me." She didn't meet his eyes.

"Why don't you go pack a couple of bags—anything you'll need for the next week or two—then I'll drive you to the lake."

"I really don't want to put your mother to any trouble—"

"My mother lives for this kind of thing," he said firmly.

Melissa looked at him through narrowed eyes, as if gauging whether or not he was telling the truth. Finally she relaxed, giving a short nod as she tucked the puppy under her arm and headed around the house to the front entrance.

"What the hell was that?" Blake asked as soon as she was out of earshot.

"What?"

"Since when do you take women home to your mother?"

"She's just an old friend."

"Y'all were never friends," Perry shot over his shoulder.

"She helped me with my calculus once," Aaron defended. "What's the big deal? Mom lives to take in strays."

"Strays? Nice, Cooper. Real nice." Perry made a face.

"You know what I mean."

"I'm beginning to think I do." Blake flashed a grin at Perry. "Cooper's homed in on a new target."

"Not his usual type, but maybe he's in the mood for something different," Perry agreed.

Aaron walked away, leaving the pair of grinning idiots behind. Was that really how people saw him? Even his friends? Sure, he'd spent a lot of years viewing women as conquests, especially back in his football days. But those days were long over. Just because he avoided long-term relationships didn't mean he was some sort of predator.

Did it?

He shook off the question as he neared the front of the house, flipping open his phone. His mother answered on the second ring. "Hi, Mom, it's me. I need your help."

As he'd expected, his mother was happy to take in Melissa for as long as needed. "Be sure to tell her not to worry about buying a lot of groceries. I just stocked the pantry with staples last week," Beth Cooper said. "And if she likes fish, Hannah and Riley just filled my freezer with a huge mess of winter crappie, so there's plenty to go around."

Aaron grinned at the phone. "Okay. I'll tell her."

As he hung up, he spotted Melissa coming out the front door, dragging two heavy-looking bags with her. Jasper was on a leash at her heels, dancing around her in a frenzy of puppy energy, threatening to trip her up.

Aaron hurried forward and relieved her of the bags. She looked up at him, her blue eyes wary. Suddenly, the puppy gave a sharp bark and dashed behind her, tangling with her legs just as she started to take a step. Losing balance, she pitched forward.

Aaron dropped the bags and caught her, wrapping his arms around her to steady her. Her breath heated the skin of his neck and he felt a dizzying flood of raw male awareness.

"Hey, Aaron!" Blake's voice, coming around the side of the house, broke the spell. "We've got something."

"I'll be right back." He released her and headed toward the back of the house. But he wasn't surprised when Melissa ignored his implied request to stay put, grabbing the puppy and tucking him into her arms as she hurried to catch up.

Perry and Blake were both crouched by the house, gazing up at a section of charred wiring, when Aaron and Melissa reached the backyard. Perry glanced up as they neared. "Definitely looks like the generator caught fire and set this side of the house on fire."

"So, not arson after all?"

"I said it looks that way. Doesn't mean that's what happened." Perry motioned Aaron nearer. Melissa stayed close enough that Aaron could feel her warmth against his side when they both bent to look at what Perry was pointing out with the beam of his flashlight. "See these wires?"

Aaron followed his gesture and saw the protective covering of the main power input cable had burned away, leaving the charred wires exposed. "What am I looking at?"

"Those wires have been cut, not burned," Perry answered. "The fire burned away the protective layer or you'd be able to see the cut more clearly."

Aaron felt Melissa's hand grab his arm. He turned to find her gazing at him, her face milk-pale in the ambient glow from the firemen's flashlights. To his surprise, while she looked afraid, she didn't look surprised.

Perry cleared his throat. "Someone definitely set this fire on purpose."

Chapter Two

Melissa felt all four gazes on her as Aaron and the other men waited for her reaction. Her skin crawled at their scrutiny. She'd made a career out of being a background player, the driven worker bee behind the scenes who got impossible things done but stayed out of the spotlight when it came time for accolades. She didn't know how she was supposed to react, what she could do to ease the suspicion she saw in Deputy Clayton's eyes or the curiosity in Perry Blake's expression.

She almost blurted out, "I didn't do it," until she realized a denial would make her look guiltier than silence.

Aaron Cooper spoke first. "Do you know why anyone would set your house on fire?"

She was grateful to find his expression devoid of suspicion. "I don't know." She wasn't the sort of person who aroused murderous passions. She hadn't had a real boyfriend since law school, didn't sleep with married men or make cutthroat business deals. She was just a midlevel attorney at a small law firm in a small Alabama city.

Who also defends women whose husbands and boyfriends like to knock them around.

Aaron seemed to catch the change in her expression. "You do know something."

Her stomach tightened with a mixture of anger and alarm.

She'd raised a few murderous passions in her pro bono work, hadn't she? From men with hair trigger tempers and violent tendencies.

"No," she said aloud.

There it was. The hint of suspicion she'd been waiting for in Aaron Cooper's expression.

She couldn't tell him about her pro bono work. It would expose her clients. She worked hard to protect them from their brutal spouses and boyfriends, to hide them from further danger and give them chances at good lives. The last thing any of them needed was cops nosing around in their pasts to find a suspect in an arson that had caused only a minor amount of damage.

"You said you saw someone moving around outside your house," Deputy Blake said, skepticism oozing from every word.

Aaron looked at Blake. "What?"

"I couldn't unlock the dead bolt on the front door." Melissa was glad to focus on something that might help Aaron. She hated lying, even if she'd had too many opportunities to hone the skill over the years. "I saw a shadow through the window, moving out of view, like someone going around the corner of the porch."

"What about when you got outside?" Aaron asked.

"I didn't see anyone. But there was a twig or something like that wedged into the front door lock from the outside."

"We don't know if it's actually connected to the fire," Blake said. "We got a few calls last night about wedges being put into locks. One of the complainants said she saw some kids running away just before she discovered the vandalism."

"Maybe they graduated to something more destructive."

"Pretty big step, from petty mischief to attempted murder," Blake pointed out.

"I'm not a shrink. I don't have to know what motivated the jerks. I just have to prove they did it," Aaron said.

"Maybe they cut the electricity as a prank," Melissa suggested. "Maybe it accidentally made a spark, igniting leftover gasoline in the generator?"

"How much gas was in the generator?" Perry asked.

She looked at him, wondering when the class clown she remembered had grown up to be this serious-faced firefighter looking at her with hard skepticism. "I don't think it could be much," she admitted. "Less than a cup. It emptied the last time I used it, and I don't add gasoline until I need it."

"You don't store the gas back here by the house, do you?" Perry asked.

"No. I keep it in the shed." Melissa pointed to the small work shed about twenty yards behind the house, near the edge of the woods that formed the border of her property.

Perry looked at Aaron. "There are signs of an accelerant, probably gasoline, in the burn patterns here. The state's arson investigation team could tell us more. Should we call them in?"

Aaron looked from Perry to Melissa. "Yeah," he said finally. "Let's call them in."

Melissa's heart sank. "I don't want you to investigate it. Nobody was hurt. I won't even make an insurance claim. Let's just leave this alone, okay?"

What was left of the compassion in Aaron's expression disappeared, corroded by undiluted cynicism. "You're a lawyer, right? You know we can't do that."

She was afraid he was going to say that. "Okay, fine. Investigate." She tightened her grip on Jasper, who'd started to whine. "Tell your mother I appreciate the offer but it's best I just find a hotel—"

Aaron caught her arm as she turned away, his strong grip just shy of painful. "The offer of the guest house stands."

She pulled her arm away, glaring at him. What, now that he saw her as a suspect, he thought he could manhandle her any way he pleased? Maybe the whole reason he wanted her at his mom's place was to make it easier to keep an eye on her.

But at this point, she was so tired and stressed she wouldn't have protested if he'd suggested an ankle monitor to track her whereabouts. She just wanted to bathe off the soot in a scalding shower, crawl into a warm bed and sleep for a week.

"Can we go now?" she asked impatiently.

"Yeah, we can go." None of the earlier gentleness remained in his deep voice. He was angry with her, clearly, and in no mood to pretend civility. Or gentleness.

He nudged her toward the driveway when she started up the cobblestone walk to retrieve her suitcases. "I'll get them. You go get in the blue truck." He pulled a set of keys from his pocket and pushed a button. Lights came on at the end of the driveway, slanting light across Aaron's grim features.

She felt annoyance flood her system. "I'd rather drive my own car."

He gave her a considering look. "You're tired and you're shaking. You don't need to be driving. I'll get a deputy to bring your car to the marina tomorrow."

Picking her battles, Melissa relented, trudging through the frost-limned grass to an enormous blue pickup truck sprawled across the mouth of her driveway. "Feel free to pee on his upholstery," she muttered to Jasper as she put him on the small bench seat behind the front bucket seats.

He sniffed the length of the bench as she pulled herself wearily into the passenger seat and shut the door behind her. The truck's cab was warm compared to the bitter cold outside. It smelled better than she expected, too—spicy, a little masculine.

Like Aaron Cooper himself, a traitorous teenage voice whispered in her head.

Melissa tucked her legs up and rested her chin on her knees, gazing through the windshield at Aaron as he lifted her suitcases as if they were lunchboxes. He may have left his football career behind, but he still looked good, she noted grudgingly. He'd been leaner in high school, but the extra flesh seemed to be all muscle.

Too bad he was such a bully.

Aaron heaved the suitcases into the truck bed, where they landed with gentle thuds. Circling to the driver's side, he opened the cab door and looked over the seat at her.

For a second, the suspicion in his eyes melted, revealing sympathy. He shrugged off his thick brown leather jacket and handed it across the seat to her. "Here, put that on. And buckle up."

He belted himself in while Melissa pulled the enormous jacket around her. It swallowed her whole, enveloping her in the same heady scent that filled the cab of his truck. She held her breath, holding that scent inside her for a moment. She felt sixteen all over again, tongue-tied and hopelessly infatuated with the star football player who barely even knew she was alive.

But a quick glance at Aaron Cooper's stony profile dragged her back to the present reality. She was temporarily homeless, frozen half-solid and apparently the prime suspect in a case of arson. And Aaron was a big, pushy guy who probably wouldn't think twice about twisting arms to get his way.

Lovely. Just lovely.

"Do you honestly think I set my own house on fire with my dog and myself inside?" she asked.

Aaron shot her a sidelong look. "I think you're keeping something from me."

"That's not what I asked."

He shrugged. "Lies make me antsy."

"I haven't lied."

He looked her way again. "Why did you want us to drop the case, Ms. Draper?"

The cool formality of his tone stung her, even though she knew it shouldn't. They were strangers, really. Passing in the halls and a few classes together didn't constitute a friendship.

Not that she wanted Aaron Cooper as a friend anyway. She'd known entirely too many men in her life who didn't know how to keep their hands—or their fists—to themselves.

She turned her face away from him and gazed out the passenger window, remaining quiet.

"I rest my case," Aaron said.

She bit back a protest. Anything she said in her defense would only pique Aaron's interest more. He was probably going to find out about her pro bono work sooner or later, but the longer it took, the more time she'd have to warn the women she worked with that scrutiny might be headed their way.

And maybe, if she could figure out which of the many violent men who'd threatened her over the years was the one who'd set fire to her house, she could tip off Aaron and put an end to the whole mess before he had to bother her clients.

The women she worked with had lived in sheer hell for years before making their escape. The last thing they needed was a nosy deputy dragging them back through hell all over again.

BY MIDMORNING, the day had warmed to the low fifties with bright sunlight to ward off the chill. The living room of the guest cottage was cozy and warm, morning sunlight through the front windows casting a cheerful glow across the homey furniture. Aaron found himself fighting the urge to stretch out on the sofa and take a nap.

Melissa and her puppy had disappeared into one of the bedrooms soon after they'd arrived, staying awake only long enough for a quick shower and the breakfast of eggs and toast Aaron's mother had had waiting for them when they walked through the door to the lakeside cabin.

His mother, Beth, had also put fresh sheets on the beds and turned up the central heating to a cozy warmth. After Melissa had gone to bed, Beth had stayed a few minutes to talk to him, managing to glean the basics of Melissa's plight from him with a few subtle, well-aimed questions.

"You don't seriously think that poor girl tried to burn her own house down, do you?" His mother's tone of voice had made him feel as if he were a complete creep to entertain the notion for a second.

He'd been relieved to admit he didn't think Melissa had set the fire. But he hadn't told his mother his strong feeling that Melissa knew who had.

The expression on her face when Perry had told them the fire had been set deliberately hadn't been shock. It had been fear, liberally tinged with a strange sort of fatalism, as if she'd been waiting for just such a thing to happen.

So as he finished up calls to the office to brief his commander and get a few investigative balls rolling, he found himself wondering why Melissa Draper had been so unsurprised to hear someone had tried to kill her.

The soft click of the bedroom door down the hallway gave him time to school his features into a cool mask of professionalism. He waited until he heard her pad quietly into the living room before he turned to look at her.

His breath hitched halfway into his lungs. He forced himself to breathe slowly and deliberately despite the sudden, unexpected pounding of his heart. She wasn't what he'd call pretty, exactly—she never had been. Her forehead was too wide, her blue eyes too large, her lips too bow-shaped, her skin too milky pale. Her dark hair had always been straight and shapeless, though instead of letting the straight locks hang down over her shoulders she now wore it pulled back into a sleek ponytail.

She wore a pair of faded jeans just tight enough to reveal a nice pair of legs and a loose-fitting gray T-shirt that concealed too much for him to get a good idea what the rest of her body looked like. Unfortunately, his mind seemed determined to fill in the blanks all by itself.

"I thought you'd be gone." Her sleep-raspy voice hit like a jolt of caffeine. He instantly focused on her, from the faint scent of shampoo in her still-damp hair to the way her lips parted to reveal a flash of perfect white teeth.

He was reacting to her like some sex-starved loser who hadn't gotten lucky in a decade. And that definitely wasn't him. What the hell was wrong with him?

He liked tough, driven women who embraced his no-promises, no-regrets idea of relationships with as much enthusiasm as he always had. He sure as hell didn't play with the hearts of women who looked as breakable as Melissa Draper.

She'd said something, he reminded himself, trying to gather his scattered thoughts to remember her remark. "I'm working here," he answered, appalled when he stumbled over his words. Clearing his throat, he dragged his attention back to the notes he'd been making for the report he'd type up when he got back to the office. "I thought I'd wait until you woke up."

"I'm up," she said.

"Trying to get rid of me?"

She gave him an odd look and moved to sit stiffly on the

chair across from the sofa where he sat. She looked nervous, he noted, but he didn't think it had anything to do with whatever secrets she was keeping. "Is my car here yet?"

He frowned. "You're not thinking of leaving."

She met his frown with a scowl of her own. "Am I under arrest? I must have missed the Miranda warning."

"You're not under arrest."

"Yet."

He pressed his lips together, annoyed—at her for being so stubborn and confrontational and with himself for the way his heart was pounding with excitement because she was sitting close enough that he could smell her soap-and-water scent every time he took a breath.

He hadn't been on a date in a while, thanks to his recent promotion at the Sheriff's Department and all the catching up he had to do on current cases. Clearly, he needed to remedy that problem, pretty damned pronto.

But he was finding it harder these days to find a woman who really sparked his interest. Wasn't that really the problem, more than the lack of time?

He wondered how much it had to do with the changes in his own family. Four marriages in the last three years, all of them deliriously happy, at least from the outside looking in—they'd been enough to force him to take a second look at the way he'd chosen to live his life over the past few years.

He'd come to believe that true, lasting love—the kind his parents shared—was the exception, not the rule. He'd seen people destroy each other in the name of love.

He'd seen people destroy themselves—

"Is my car here or not?" Melissa's impatient voice interrupted him.

"It's out front." His voice emerged in a low growl. "Deputy Clayton dropped it off about an hour ago. You're free to go anywhere you want, as long as you don't leave the area. We're going to have more questions for you."

He grabbed his phone and his notebook, stuffing both in the pocket of his leather jacket. The faint smell of smoke assailed his nostrils, reminding him how she'd looked earlier that morning in the cab of his truck, all big blue eyes and shaky bravado. He'd better run by his house to get another jacket, he decided, or he might not get any work done the rest of the day.

"You're leaving?" She trailed him to the door.

He paused in the doorway, surprised to find her standing so close. "I need to type up the report and check on some other cases we're working. If you need anything, give me a call." He leaned forward, telling himself it wasn't to get a better whiff of her heady scent. "And if you suddenly remember who might have wanted to hurt you, you know where to find me."

Her eyes met his, full of secrets. When she didn't answer, he forced himself to turn and leave.

In the cab of his truck, he took a couple of long, deep breaths. Grabbing his phone from his pocket, he dialed the number of the Betancourt Law Firm in Maybridge and asked for Tina Lewis, a lawyer he'd gone out with a few months earlier.

"Hey, Tina, it's Aaron," he said when she answered. "What are you doing tomorrow night?"

MELISSA'S BOSS, Carter Morgan, insisted she take the whole day off. "You've probably got a million things to take care of. Where are you now—at home?"

"I'm staying at a friend's house on Gossamer Lake." Melissa glanced at Jasper, who was whining softly at the front door of the cottage. "Are you sure you don't need me to come in? With Alice off this week, you'll be shorthanded." She willed Carter to say yes. Hanging around the cottage all day, waiting for Aaron Cooper to decide to arrest her after all, would drive her insane.

Besides, she wasn't sure she could even trust him.

"You don't have any cases going to court this week. Take the rest of the week off, too, if you need it," Carter insisted, his tone almost fatherly. "You can come back fresh and prepared on Monday."

"I'll be there tomorrow," Melissa insisted. She hung up the phone with a growl of frustration. So much for using work to distract herself today.

Of course, there was always Domestic Crisis Center work to be done. She had a list of clients she could call to check on. There were two child custody cases pending, and another woman had taken a restraining order out on her boyfriend recently. Melissa should probably check with her to see if he was complying with the order.

She'd made a couple of calls and was about to check on the woman with the restraining order when Jasper jumped into her lap and started whining. "I guess you're about ready to go outside, aren't you, big boy?" She scratched behind his soft, floppy ears and set him on the floor, tucking her phone into the pocket of her jeans.

Outside, with the day creeping toward noon, the temperature had risen high enough that the cardigan she'd donned before leaving the cottage was sufficient to keep her comfortable. She was tempted to settle down in the weathered wooden rocker on the cottage's front porch to make the rest of her calls. What a difference from the previous night's frigid cold and discomfort.

Jasper began to bark wildly, his tail wagging with canine joy. It took Melissa a few seconds to spot what Jasper had clearly seen moments before: a pretty young woman walking up the path to the house, a baby on her hip.

Aaron's sister Hannah, Melissa realized as the woman came closer. She'd been a couple of years behind Melissa in school. Like Aaron, Hannah had moved in a different social circle, but Melissa's memory of the youngest Cooper was positive. In high school, at least, Hannah had been the rare kind of person who'd related easily to anyone she'd met.

Hannah looked a lot like her brother Aaron, though smaller and much more feminine. Her eyes were green, not gray like Aaron's, but they had the same ridiculously long, dark lashes and bright inquisitiveness. And the woman's square jaw was also clearly a Cooper trait.

"Hi, Melissa." She smiled brightly, ignoring Jasper's barks. "I don't know if you remember me—I'm Hannah Cooper. Well, Patterson now. Aaron's sister." She grinned at the puppy. "And this must be Jasper."

"I remember you." Melissa smiled back at her, surprised to feel instantly at ease. "And yes, Mr. Manners here is Jasper. Who really needs to stop barking anytime now," she added with a hint of frustration in her voice.

"Jasper, hush," Hannah said in a forceful tone. The puppy quieted down immediately, gazing up at Hannah with a look of sheer adoration, his tail wagging merrily.

"How did you do that?" Melissa asked, incredulous.

"You just have to let them know you mean business. Sort of like dealing with brothers, too."

The baby, who'd handled Jasper's yapping without a whimper, began to cry when the puppy stopped barking. Hannah laughed. "Poor Cody—the only thing that scares him is peace and quiet. Luckily, he doesn't get much of that around here."

Melissa shook off her darker musing. "He's adorable. Is he yours?"

Hannah beamed. "Yeah, he's my little wrangler. My husband wanted to name him after a town back in Wyoming. That's where Riley's from."

"Oh, right. I heard you'd married a cowboy."

Hannah's grin broadened, but before she could answer, Melissa's cell phone rang. Melissa grabbed it, murmuring a quick apology to Hannah. She noted with amusement that the phone's loud ring had quieted Cody immediately.

"Melissa Draper."

"Melissa, it's Dinah Harris."

Melissa's amusement faded quickly. Dinah was one of her clients, a woman whose husband Terry had a nasty temper. Melissa had helped Dinah get a restraining order against Terry a couple of months earlier. "Hi, Dinah. Is something wrong?"

"I need to talk to you. Can you get here before noon?" Though nothing she said denoted alarm, Dinah's voice sounded tight and worried. Melissa didn't like the sound of it.

"I'll be right there." She hung up and looked down at Jasper, who was still gazing lovingly at Hannah.

"Everything okay?" Hannah asked.

"A client needs to see me. She sounds worried, so I need to go. But I forgot about Jasper. I don't want to leave him alone in the cottage in case he has an accident."

"Leave him with Cody and me. We'll take him with us down to the bait shop to visit Mom and Dad. He'll love it." Hannah reached for Jasper's leash.

"Are you sure?" Melissa asked.

"Positive." Hannah took the leash with a genuine smile. "I'll see if I can teach him a few tricks before you get back." She started off down the path toward the lakeside marina, Jasper trotting along beside her without so much as a backward glance.

"Traitor," Melissa muttered with a grin, but her humor

fled as soon as she got behind the wheel of her Volkswagen. The worry in Dinah's voice might mean nothing.

But if Terry Harris was back in her life, it could very well mean murder.

Chapter Three

"She's squeaky clean." Aaron's brother-in-law and fellow deputy Riley Patterson handed Aaron a file folder. "Her insurance agent says she barely has enough coverage on the house to pay for the repairs. She's never shown any signs of being an attention seeker. Damned if I can see where she had a motive to burn down her own house."

Aaron had figured as much. It was more likely that someone else had lit the match to torch the place. But who? And why? The same factors that made Melissa Draper an unlikely suspect for arson made her an unlikely victim as well.

Still, she clearly knew more about the fire than she was admitting. It was time he asked her, point blank, to tell him what she was hiding.

He grabbed the phone and dialed the number to the cottage. After five rings, the answering machine picked up. Stifling a mild curse, he left a message, wishing he'd thought to get her cell phone number before he'd left that morning. "Is her cell number in this file somewhere?" he asked Riley.

"Check her initial statement."

Aaron found the number and tried it. No answer on the cell phone, either. He left a message there as well, grumbling as he hung up.

"Maybe she walked down to the bait shop," Riley suggested.

Aaron tried the number to his parents' shop. His sister Hannah answered on the second ring. "Cooper Cove Marina."

"Hey, Skipper, is Melissa Draper there?" He knew he wouldn't have to explain his query. His mother would have told Hannah all about her houseguest the second his sister walked into the bait shop.

"She left the cottage about twenty minutes ago," Hannah told him. "I think she got a call from a client or something."

A client? She was trying to work today?

"She seemed troubled when she left." Hannah's voice went serious. "She tried to hide it, but the call changed her whole mood."

Worry nudged Aaron in the gut. What if the call was connected to the secret she was keeping about the arson? "If she calls or shows back up, call me immediately," Aaron told her. "Tell Mom and Dad to do the same."

"Is she in some kind of trouble?" Hannah asked.

"Probably not." Even he could hear the lack of conviction in his voice.

After he rang off, he called the county dispatcher and requested that they flag any calls from Melissa Draper's cell and home phone numbers and let Aaron know about them.

"Hey, Aaron, check this out," Riley called from his desk.

Aaron crossed to his brother-in-law's side and looked over his shoulder at the computer screen. On the screen was a police report from the department's archives, a domestic disturbance call from a couple of years earlier.

The complainant was Melissa Draper, who lived at an address on Tuckahaw Road.

"This is the third similar report I've found," Riley said.

"Three domestic disturbances, three calls from Melissa Draper."

Three different couples involved, Aaron saw as Riley clicked through the screens. Melissa was never listed as a victim, just the person reporting the disturbance.

"That's strange," Aaron murmured.

"You said she's a lawyer, right?"

"Right. Corporate law—contracts, powers of attorney—"

"Maybe she does pro bono cases on the side." Riley crossed to the file cabinets, rifling through the top drawer of the cabinet nearest the wall and emerging with a manila folder. He scanned the contents quickly, recognition spreading across his face. "I knew her name was familiar. She was the lawyer of record for the victim in a domestic abuse case I investigated back in the fall, one of my first cases after making investigator." Riley handed the file to Aaron. "I met her before the trial. Seemed nice. A little quiet. But man, when she got that abusive son of a bitch on the stand, she turned into a tiger. Ripped him apart. It seemed— personal, you know? Some lawyers do pro bono work for causes they care about."

"So the client she's gone to see may be an abused wife." Aaron frowned. Where there were abused wives, there were big, mean, violent husbands.

He dialed Melissa's cell phone again. Still no answer.

He was starting to get a very bad feeling.

MELISSA's cell phone vibrated against her side as she climbed the porch steps at Dinah Harris's house, the second call in the last ten minutes. Same digits on the display, but since she didn't recognize the number she let voice mail take it.

She knocked on the front door. Usually, a knock brought Dinah's two little boys running to be the first to answer. But all Melissa heard was silence.

A few seconds later, the faint tap of footsteps approached the door. It opened and Dinah Harris stood in the doorway, looking at Melissa with scared green eyes.

"What is it?" Melissa stepped forward, taking Dinah's hand. "Has Terry been back here?"

"C-come in and have some tea." Dinah grasped Melissa's hand, tugging her into the small, drab living room, her eyes glassy and wide with dread.

The hairs on Melissa's arms bristled, her inner alarm clanging a dire warning. But before she could take even a step back, someone moved out from the shadows behind the door and caught her arm in a cruel, painful grasp.

"Glad you could join us, bitch," Terry Harris murmured in her ear.

Her heart bucking wildly as a surge of sheer terror flooded her veins, she tried to jerk away from him. But he only tightened his grip, his fingers digging brutally into her arm.

"No, you don't," he growled, dragging her through the doorway leading into the kitchen.

Melissa had always known a day like this would come. In some ways she'd been preparing for it for years. Self-defense training, therapy to build the emotional toughness to handle confrontations—even criminal profiling courses so she'd have the mental edge in a dangerous situation.

But no amount of forethought could keep her adrenal glands in check or erase the sometimes crippling memories now flooding her brain with a poisonous dose of unadulterated fear.

Terry pushed her into the wall next to the refrigerator. Her shoulder slammed into the sheetrock, pain flashing through her chest at the jarring impact. He didn't give her time to do more than wince, advancing until he was inches from her face. His breath was fetid, laced with alcohol and a hint of marijuana smoke, but the enormous size of his pupils, black pools rimmed with only a sliver of blue, hinted he might be amped up on crystal meth. "No wonder a nosy bitch like you ain't got a man of her own. Who'd have you? But that don't give you no cause to mess with me and Dinah."

"You're right, Terry. I'll just go now, okay? Message received." She kept her tone reasonable, struggling for calm and focus. She tried to slide sideways away from him, but he shot his arm out, trapping her in place.

"Terry, please don't—" Dinah grabbed his arm. Terry wheeled around, backhanding his wife. She cried out, stumbling back against the sink counter.

"Shut up and let me handle this!" Terry whirled around as Melissa tried to duck under his arm, grabbing her neck in one big, rough hand to pin her to the wall. "Stay put."

Melissa froze in place, her pulse roaring in her ears. Her legs trembled wildly as she tried to remain completely still, aware that no amount of logic or reason was going to get through to a man so steeped in drugs and rage. But if she could keep him from killing her in the next few minutes, she might get the opportunity to wield the small vial of pepper spray tucked in the pocket of her jacket.

She was shaking so hard that it took a couple of seconds to realize the vibration she felt against her hip was coming from her cell phone. Her fingers itched to reach into her pocket and answer the call, but she didn't dare make a move while Terry was watching.

But a moment later, Terry turned his head to check on Dinah's location, perhaps afraid that she might make a move against him while his back was turned, though she sat in a crumpled, defeated heap in front of the sink, crying softly, her eyes averted. His inattention gave Melissa the chance she needed.

She slipped her hand into her pocket and pushed the call button on her phone, returning the call to whomever had just tried to ring her, then wrapped her fist around the pepper spray canister, flipping open the safety top.

Terry wheeled back around to her, squeezing her throat. For a second, black spots swam in front of her eyes and a dull roar deafened her to all but the sound of her rushing blood. Finally his grip loosened, and sound and sight returned with dizzying clarity, along with a raw ache in her bruised throat.

"You don't have a man to teach you how things are supposed to be, do you? You don't have no respect for what's on us. Gotta make money to keep the house and feed the whining, ungrateful brats and a worthless, shiftless woman who treats you like a workhorse. Can't even get a decent supper on the table on time." He whipped around and looked at his wife, uttering a cruel epithet that made Melissa flinch, even though she'd heard it many times before from any number of angry, violent men.

His grip loosened more, giving Melissa the opening she needed. She pulled the pepper spray from her pocket and held it out in front of her, ready when Terry Harris turned back around to face her again. His eyes widened as he spotted the canister, giving him no defense when she pressed the trigger and squirted a burning stream into his face.

AARON gripped the steering wheel tightly, horror flooding him in cold greasy waves. Over the cell phone headset, instead of Melissa's voice, he heard a muffled male voice spew pure venom, vicious and cruel. Suddenly, the voice cut off with a bark of pain, and Aaron had to jerk the steering wheel quickly to keep his truck from plunging down an embankment to his right.

He listened with growing panic, trying to make sense of what he was hearing. The bark of pain turned into howls of agony, punctuated by the sound of footsteps, still oddly muted. Was the phone in Melissa's pocket?

Why hadn't she said anything yet?

Finally, Melissa's voice broke through the chaos. "Where are the kids?" The urgency in her raspy voice made his gut ache. Where was she? What was going on? Was she hurt?

What kids?

"Go," another woman's voice answered, raw with tears. "I ain't leavin'."

So Riley had been right. She was with one of the abuse victims she worked with. He tried to remember what Hannah had told him about the phone call Melissa had received. His sister had said Melissa seemed worried but not panicky.

Had she walked into a siege, unaware?

The howls of pain continued in the background, behind the women's low murmurs. Just before the first cry, he'd heard a sort of hissing sound. Pepper spray?

Pepper spray might slow the assailant down, but it wouldn't be enough to stop him once the first wave of burning settled down. Melissa had to get out of there, and soon.

"If you stay here, he'll kill you." Melissa's voice rose with urgency. "Where are the kids, Dinah?"

"Just get out of here," Dinah answered. Aaron heard a tone in her voice he'd heard before, too many times.

Hopelessness.

Get out, Melissa, he silently urged. *You can't save her.*

He heard a crashing sound over the phone, and his nerves jumped wildly. He almost sagged with relief when he heard Melissa speak again. "Are the kids in the house?"

"Just go!" Dinah's voice rose hysterically. There was a soft thud and he thought he heard a small gasp from Melissa, but he couldn't be sure. The sound of the yelling man hadn't seemed to get any closer.

Suddenly that noise faded, replaced by the faint sound of

running footsteps. A few seconds later, the footsteps changed, grew hollow. A rustling sound, loud enough to make him wince, was followed quickly by Melissa's breathless voice, loud and direct into the phone. "Call 911. Domestic assault in progress at 223 Old Borland Road in Gossamer Ridge."

"Are you out of there? Get out of there!" he responded, his heart hammering against his chest wall. "Melissa?"

"Aaron?" Her voice cracked. He heard the sound of a door opening, then slamming shut. A soft "snick" of doors locking. "I'm in my car. Doors locked."

Her previous words sliced through the haze of relief. Old Borland Road was about three minutes away. He gunned the truck engine. "Are you okay? What happened?"

"I'm okay. Just get here. I'll be waiting at the highway turnoff. And you're going to need backup."

"Let me call it in." He grabbed the radio. "I need two cruisers. And get Riley Patterson out here."

Melissa's voice rang in his ear. "Have them stop at the turnoff."

He added that direction to his call to dispatch. "What else do we need to know?" he asked Melissa.

She told him about her visit to her client in short, hoarse sentences. He could tell from her breathlessness and the shaky sound of her voice that she was suffering from mild shock.

"Did he hit you?" Aaron asked, his voice strangled.

"No. He—he manhandled me a little, but I'm okay."

"I'll get paramedics to look you over—"

"No, I'm fine," she insisted, coughing a little as her voice rose. "I'm a lot more worried about Dinah and the kids."

"How many kids?"

"Two boys, five and seven. I didn't see them."

"Is Harris ever abusive to them?"

"Not so far. It's all been directed at Dinah. But they should have been there. Dinah doesn't like to leave them with other people. She's afraid Terry will try to grab them."

Her fear was contagious. Aaron's head filled with images that made him want to pull over to the side of the road and throw up his lunch. "Did you see any signs of a struggle? Any blood? Did you smell—"

"God!"

"I'm sorry, but we need to know what we're heading into. Did you see anything to suggest the kids might be there?"

The sound of her Volkswagen's engine died, and there was almost perfect silence on the other end of the line.

"Melissa?"

"I didn't see anything," she said in a low voice. "I didn't hear…anything."

Like kids playing in a back room, Aaron thought. Hard to play when—

"She sounded so defeated," Melissa said. "Like she'd given up. She didn't even respond to my question about the kids."

He pushed the dark images out of his head. One thing at a time. "Let's just get Harris out of that house, and then we'll deal with finding the kids." As he heard sirens in the distance, he saw the turnoff to Old Borland Road looming down the highway. "I'm almost there, Melissa. And backup's on the way. Can you hear the sirens?"

"Yeah." Her voice shook.

He slowed into the turn, spotting her Volkswagen on the gravel shoulder ahead. He pulled up in front of her and cut the engine, halfway out the door before the sound died. He rounded the truck bed and headed for the driver's door of the GTI.

Before he reached her, she pushed open the car door, stumbling a little as she emerged from behind the wheel. His breath caught at the sight of the ugly purple marks on her throat and the gray pallor in her shell-shocked face.

She locked gazes with him for a moment, her eyes huge and haunted. Then she flung herself into his arms.

"I DIDN'T SEE or hear the kids," Melissa said.

Aaron stood beside her, his hand under her elbow to support her, although she'd stopped shaking soon after she'd hurled herself against him a few minutes earlier. After his reaction to her that morning, he hadn't been surprised by his body's surge of pleasure at the feel of her pressed hard against him. But the rage that surged through him when he examined her injuries had caught him completely off guard.

It was taking most of his self-control to stay still while she briefed the deputies he'd flagged down before they raced into a potential hostage situation with sirens blazing.

"As far as you could see, it was just Harris and his wife?" Blake Clayton asked. He was one of the four deputies sent by dispatch when Aaron had put in the call about the assault.

Melissa nodded. She pressed her body back against his, as if seeking his warmth and strength. He tightened his grip on her elbow, his thumb sliding comfortingly against her arm.

"You said you think he could be high?" Aaron asked.

"I know he's done crystal meth in the past," she answered. "He's acting high. Completely out of control."

"Was he armed?" he asked, kicking himself for taking so long to ask the most pertinent question.

"I didn't see any kind of weapon. I don't know." Melissa looked up at him. "Dinah never mentioned weapons before. I think he just uses his fists."

His fists were weapons enough, Aaron thought blackly, his gaze dropping to the darkening bruises on Melissa's throat.

"We have to assume the children are still in the house, even if you didn't see them." He struggled to keep his anger in check. "We need to get him outside the house if possible."

"Maybe I should go back there," Melissa suggested.

Aaron's gut clenched. "No."

She frowned. "He's angry with me. I hurt him. It could be enough to get him outside."

"He may have a weapon. I'm not putting you in harm's way."

"I didn't see a gun, and anything less than that, you could get to him before he got to me."

He caught her arm and turned her to face him, loosening his grip when he saw her wince. He smoothed his hand over her arm where he'd grabbed her. "Someone already tried to set your house on fire," he said more quietly.

She gave him a dark look. "Y'all thought that was me."

"If Terry Harris set that fire, he obviously wanted you dead. I won't give him a chance to get it right this time." He eyed the other deputies, who were looking at him for direction. Would he ever get used to being the one with authority? "So, how else can we get Harris out of the house?"

"Do we know anything about his family? Mother, father—maybe a sibling?" asked Kendrick Dell, an earnest young rookie fresh out of the county police academy. Aaron gave him a quick look of approval, and the young man beamed with pride.

"His mother works at the chicken processing plant in Cedar Creek," Melissa offered, referring to a town fifteen minutes to the east, across the county line. "I think they're close. She was the only one in the family still speaking to him."

"Would she help us arrest him, though?" Blake asked.

"She's not blind to his problems. She didn't stand in Dinah's way at the custody hearing. He seems to listen to her."

Aaron turned to Kendrick. "Get on the horn to Sunshine Processing in Cedar Creek. Ask for—" He looked at Melissa.

"Mary Mullins," she supplied.

"Tell Mrs. Mullins we'll send a car to pick her up. Don't scare her. Just tell her we need her to talk to her son. Then go pick her up."

Kendrick headed to the patrol car.

Riley Patterson arrived, to Aaron's relief. Even though Aaron had more seniority with the sheriff's department than his brother-in-law, Riley had more experience as an investigator. He'd been a deputy chief in Wyoming, taking the pay cut and the loss of rank when he chose to move to Alabama to be with Hannah. Riley was damned good at the job, and Aaron's ego wasn't so big that he couldn't look to the man for help.

He pulled Riley aside and caught him up on what had happened. "Melissa thinks Harris's mother may be able to get through to him. Kendrick's gone to pick her up."

Nodding approvingly, Riley looked at Melissa, who leaned against the side of Aaron's truck, her arms wrapped tightly around herself. "She okay?"

"Seems to be. He did a number on her neck, but she got herself out of there in pretty good shape." She looked scared and sad. Aaron squelched the urge to give her a hug and forced his gaze back to his brother-in-law, lowering his voice. "I'm worried about the Harris kids. Melissa says the mother doesn't usually let them out of her sight. But Melissa didn't see or hear them in the house."

Riley's expression went grim. "Not good."

"I keep picturing—" Aaron couldn't say the words aloud.

"I know." Riley laid a hand on Aaron's shoulder. "But I took a quick look at Harris's file before I came out here. He doesn't have a record of hurting the kids."

"Ordinary guys snap and take out their whole families." Aaron glanced at Melissa again. "We can't wait here forever."

"We can have the A.B.I. hostage negotiation guys here in an hour. Maybe sooner by helicopter, if you think the situation is bad enough." Riley followed Aaron's gaze. "Melissa Draper is the closest thing we have to a fly on the wall in there. She knows the lay of the house, right? The players?"

Riley was right. Melissa was their best source. He should be grilling her, picking her brain for anything she might know that they could use to their advantage. He shouldn't be trying to protect her at all costs—that wasn't his job.

He crossed to her side. "You said you want to help us."

She gave a silent but firm nod.

Aaron pulled his notepad from his pocket. "Then walk me through that house."

Chapter Four

"He's got to be wondering why the police haven't shown up yet." Melissa watched Aaron sketch across a notepad, adding notes to the crude floor plan he'd drawn from her description.

"We can't rush in and make things worse."

"Worse than it already is?" She didn't see how the situation in the Harris house could get any grimmer.

"Uncertainty may keep him quiet, at least for a while." Aaron sounded more hopeful than confident. "And his mother will be here any minute. We're going to let her call him, see if she can talk him into leaving the house to meet her."

"He's not *that* fond of his mother."

Aaron slanted a look her way. "I don't remember your being such a pessimist."

"You don't remember me at all," she countered flatly.

"Not true. I'm pretty sure that was you who got me through honors algebra."

"That was Dina Pritchard." Idiot. Not that she was surprised. To a guy like Aaron Cooper, all the band geeks and science nerds had probably looked alike in high school.

"I know you got me through at least one class," he said.

"No, I'm the one who wouldn't let you copy my chemistry papers," she retorted. "I was never desperate enough for jock attention to stoop to cheating."

A hint of redness rose in his neck as he looked away. Was he actually embarrassed by his mistake? That would be a first.

"I still think I could get him to come outside," she murmured, looking at the drawing in his notebook.

"No," Aaron said firmly. "He'll suspect a trap."

"He'll suspect a trap if his mother suddenly calls him out of the blue. But he might buy that I'd come back alone to help Dinah. He knows how serious I am about protecting my clients, even from the police." She touched his arm, making him look at her. "I won't have to go inside. I'll tell him if he sends Dinah out unharmed, I won't call the police."

She could see Aaron considering the sense of her proposal. She could also see his fierce opposition to the idea. "I know you're trying to keep me safe, but this is your best chance of getting him out of that house voluntarily. You must know that."

"She's right." Riley Patterson, Aaron's brother-in-law, spoke up. "We can stay out of sight. We'll put a vest on her—under her coat, where he won't spot it."

Aaron frowned. "A vest can't stop everything."

"I told you he prefers using his fists." She grimaced. "You know, the personal touch."

Aaron looked up sharply at her words. "You'd have to do everything by phone. Stay back a good distance from the house."

"I'll stay back," she promised.

Aaron looked at Riley. "Do we have a vest that'll fit?"

"Grace is here—Melissa can borrow hers." Riley motioned a slim, red-haired female deputy over. She was a few inches taller than Melissa but approximately the same build.

Grace dimpled at Aaron as she handed over the vest. Once a heartbreaker, always a heartbreaker, Melissa thought blackly. Even fellow deputies couldn't resist him.

Not that she was immune herself, she had to admit as her whole body went into estrogen shock when he wrapped the vest around her torso and took his own sweet time buckling the stays.

"Okay, let's get your jacket back on," he murmured in the unconsciously sexy voice that had set dozens of female hearts into palpitations in high school, hers included. But that response was just an attack of hormones. Sexual attraction.

It certainly wasn't trust. She didn't dare trust Aaron Cooper—or any man. Instead of worrying about her libido, she should be thinking about how she was putting herself in harm's way for a woman who'd lured her to what could have been certain death if she hadn't been prepared. Victim or no victim, was Dinah Harris really worth risking her life a second time?

Yes, a small, determined voice answered as Aaron buttoned her jacket over the vest. Dinah Harris was weak because she'd had most of her moral strength beaten out of her, time and time again. *There but for the grace of God...*

"Ready?" Aaron asked, looking anything but.

She jutted her chin. "Yes."

Aaron bent close. "The edge of the property is, what? Twenty yards from the house?" At her nod, he continued. "Okay, keep that distance. Use the cell phone to call. Try to talk him out of the house."

"What if he won't come out?"

"Then we get you out of there. We'll let his mother try."

Reason wasn't going to work with Terry Harris. Not now. He was running on anger and adrenaline. Only his rage would draw him out of the safety of his house.

And she knew exactly what buttons to push.

OLD BORLAND ROAD had once been a busy thoroughfare, winding along Tuckahaw Branch from one end of the county to the other. The road had once connected Gossamer Ridge with a larger town in a neighboring county, but twenty years ago, the state had finally finished a four-lane highway that cut the trip in half so Old Borland Road had fallen into general disuse.

The Harris house stood near the halfway point between Gossamer Ridge and the county line, the nearest house a quarter mile away. Woods encroached on the property from three sides.

Aaron and Riley split up near the house, Riley circling to approach from the west, while Aaron set up closer to the property edge, behind a thick mass of kudzu that had overgrown a scrubby stand of crab apple trees just east of the Harris home.

The house itself was vintage rural Alabama, a dilapidated old farmhouse fallen into chronic disrepair. Its clapboard siding hadn't seen new paint in at least a decade, the cream color grimy, weathered and peeling in spots. Aaron felt depressed just looking at the place. He wondered what it must feel like to live inside its flaking walls, terrified of the person you'd once loved enough to marry.

They'd gone radio silent this close to the house, the teams communicating through text-messages on silenced cell phones. Aaron felt his phone vibrate and picked it up to see a message from Grace Baker.

DRAPER IN PLACE. GO?

It took a second to realize he was the one who had to make the call. He was the guy with seniority on the scene.

He typed "GO," pausing with his thumb over the send button. Once Melissa Draper arrived at the Harris driveway, any number of unpredictable events could occur, many of which were very bad. There was still time to back out.

She knows the situation. She's ready to do it. Trust her.

He pressed Send. And waited.

Melissa's Volkswagen finally appeared around the curve a hundred yards down the road and drove slowly to the edge of the Harris property. She parked on the road, aware that they'd put roadblocks at either end of the road to divert traffic.

Her movements deliberate, she stepped out of the car. Aaron saw her punch a number into her cell phone. They hadn't had time to wire her for sound, but her voice carried to his position. "Terry, it's Melissa Draper. Let me talk to Dinah."

Aaron was also close enough to hear Harris's roar of rage through the thin walls of the farmhouse.

For a moment Aaron's vision burned red with the memory of the bruises staining Melissa's creamy throat, and the urge to break the man's neck was almost more than he could handle.

He controlled himself with effort, centering his attention on Melissa's vulnerable profile. She didn't need his anger. She needed his undivided attention, focused like a laser on her precarious situation.

"I just want to know she's okay. Why don't you let her come out and talk to me?" Melissa asked.

"Why don't I come out and talk to you instead?" Terry bellowed. Aaron thought he heard the walls of the house rattle.

"If that's what you want. I'm certainly not coming in."

Nice, Aaron thought. She was leading him right into the trap she was setting.

He couldn't hear Terry's response this time, but Melissa's voice rang clearly in the cold air. "Look out the window, Terry. I came alone. No police. Dinah has always been clear about keeping the police out of her business. I have a duty to respect her wishes. You know that."

Aaron had a feeling that Dinah would forgive her for that lie, if she got out of this mess alive.

From his vantage point, he spotted the curtain moving in the front window. A man's face appeared in the pane, morning sunlight casting a glare on the glass, obscuring his features. But what Aaron did see when he lifted his binoculars to his eyes made his blood run cold.

The man held a large black handgun clutched in both hands.

Aaron's heartbeat stuttered, kicking up to a gallop. He quickly texted the information to the other teams. Riley replied back immediately. "Aiming?"

Aaron checked again. Terry had the gun pointing upward, not outward toward Melissa.

"No, Terry. Please don't do anything you can't take back." Melissa's voice had softened, but Aaron's senses seemed to be on full alert, picking up even the most subtle bits of stimuli, from the rough texture of winter-dried mulberry bushes against his cheek to the loamy odor of decaying vegetation beneath his boots. Had Harris told her about the gun, or was she able to see it from her position at the edge of the property?

"At least send Dinah out first. Do you really want this to be how she remembers you? So weak and cowardly?" The contempt in Melissa's voice caught Aaron off guard.

Was she trying to provoke Harris into hurting her?

Glass shattered. Aaron whipped his gaze from Melissa's pale profile to the front window in time to see something small and black fly out the window.

"You bitch!" Harris howled through the shattered window. He expounded on his rage in a flood of vicious epithets that set Aaron's blood to boiling.

Blake Clayton put his hand on Aaron's arm. "He just got rid of his weapon. He's not going to be able to reach her before we stop him. Stay cool."

"He may have a rifle or something like that."

"As long as he stays there yelling at her, he's not hurting his wife or going for another weapon. Let it play out. She's doing a good job with him."

Too good a job, Aaron thought blackly, expecting Harris to crash through the window any second.

"Don't put down the phone, Terry," Melissa called out, her voice firm and strong. "Dinah did what you wanted, didn't she? She called me here. You're angry at me, not her. Let her come out so I can make sure she's okay. Then you and I can talk."

Harris didn't answer. With a large section of the window broken, Aaron's view of the man was unimpeded by glare off the glass. He still hovered at the window, holding his hand up against his chest. It looked bloody—had he cut himself when he threw the gun through the window?

"Terry, come on. You're supposed to be a man. Are you afraid to come out here and face me?"

Aaron looked over at Melissa. Had she lost her mind? It was one thing to try to talk the man out, but taunting him was only going to make him that much more dangerous.

"She's got steel—"

Aaron shushed Blake as Harris yelled another stream of crude profanities at Melissa.

"Just words, Terry," Melissa called. "Afraid to face me now that I'm ready? Why don't you give it a try?"

"That's enough," Aaron growled, starting forward.

Blake grabbed him again. "Harris just disappeared."

"He could be going for another weapon. We need to get her out of here." He sent a quick text to Riley, telling him to abort the plan.

Before Riley could respond, the front door of the Harris house opened and Terry Harris strode out, moving at a dangerously fast clip.

"Go, go, go!" Aaron shouted, surging forward as Harris moved toward the pistol he'd thrown into the yard.

Aaron spared a quick look toward Melissa. She'd run back to the Volkswagen and taken cover, thank God.

He turned on the afterburners, wincing as his old knee injury twinged, and hit Harris at full speed, slamming him to the ground. The impact drove the air right of out of Harris's lungs. He gasped for breath, each attempt at respiration coming with a rattling croak.

"Let him up, let him up!" Hands grabbed Aaron's arms, tugging him away, but Aaron fought to stay where he was, pinning Harris to the ground with his forearm.

"You're suffocating him!" Riley's voice ripped through Aaron's adrenaline-fueled haze. His brother-in-law jerked him back from Harris, dragging him away.

Four other deputies immediately converged on Harris, cuffing him and hauling him to his feet.

Harris found his breath and howled across the yard at Melissa, calling her names so foul, Aaron almost pulled loose of Riley's restraining hold to go after the man again.

"Just words," Riley growled, echoing Melissa's earlier taunt. "He's in custody. We have a job to do."

Aaron struggled against the anger still boiling inside him, stunned by how close he'd just come to killing Terry Harris. If he'd held him in that choke hold another minute—

"We have to go inside, Aaron." Riley's grip gentled. "Got to see what kind of damage he did."

Aaron took a few more deep breaths, forcing his head back to the task at hand. He looked over his shoulder and found Melissa staring at him, her eyes huge in her pale face. She turned away, leaning against the side of her car.

"Let's go inside," Riley repeated.

Aaron turned and followed his brother-in-law inside the

Harris house, his mind swirling with bleak images of what horrors might lie inside.

"I'M HER ATTORNEY. I have a right to be in there with her." Melissa stood her ground with the red-haired deputy Grace, who currently barred her way into the Harris home. Aaron and Deputy Patterson had entered the house a few minutes earlier while she was still fighting off a massive wave of queasiness behind her car. But if Dinah was still alive—and Melissa prayed she was—she had a right to an attorney before the police asked her any questions.

Especially someone as reckless and out of control as Aaron Cooper was at the moment.

Aaron appeared in the doorway, filling the space completely. "You can come in," he told Melissa. "And give Grace's vest back."

She tried not to glare at him as she removed the vest, even though her mind brimmed with the violence she'd witnessed from him a few minutes earlier. No matter what Harris had done, no one had a right to throttle him to death the way Aaron had nearly done.

She was right. He was like all the others.

"Is Dinah okay?" she asked briskly.

"Seems to be." Aaron cupped her elbow.

Melissa jerked her arm away.

Aaron gave her an odd look but said nothing else as he led her into the Harris's kitchen, where Dinah sat hunched over in one of the old ladder back chairs at the table. Her face was tear-stained but unbruised, to Melissa's relief.

She crouched by Dinah's chair. "Are you all right?"

Dinah nodded, sniffling. Melissa got up and found a paper towel roll standing by the sink. She pulled off a couple of sheets and handed them to Dinah, shooting Aaron and the other deputy an indignant look. They couldn't bother to give the poor woman a napkin to wipe her eyes?

"Where are the children, Mrs. Harris?" Aaron's voice sounded deceptively gentle.

Dinah didn't answer.

Melissa put her hand on Dinah's arm. "It's okay, Dinah. He's locked up now. He can't hurt you. Any of you. Now, where are the boys?"

Dinah met her gaze, her green eyes lifeless. "They're locked in the cellar."

"Are they okay, Dinah?"

Dinah's gaze dropped. She didn't seem to hear the question, even when Melissa repeated it.

"Where's the key to the cellar, Dinah?" She tightened her grip on Dinah's arm. When she still didn't answer, Melissa looked around the kitchen until she spotted Dinah's purse lying on the floor in the corner by the refrigerator.

"See if the keys are in her purse," she told Aaron, her stomach knotting.

Aaron picked up the purse and rifled through it until he found a key ring with several keys.

"I'll show you where the cellar is." Melissa rose to her feet and led Aaron down the narrow hallway to the small door that led down to the cellar beneath the house. She tried the door. It was locked.

Aaron tried the keys one at a time. The third key worked. "You should stay here," he told Melissa.

She shook her head. "If they're still alive, they'll be terrified. They know me."

"And if they're not?"

She couldn't let herself think that way.

"Let's go."

Pocketing the keys, Aaron opened the cellar door and they headed down the stairs.

He led the way, filling the stairwell so completely that Melissa couldn't see anything ahead of them. He emerged finally at the bottom of the stairs and stopped, blocking Melissa's view of the room.

Her heart skipped a beat. Why had he stopped?

"I don't see them," he said softly.

"Let me look." She nudged his back, and he stepped aside, giving her an unobstructed view of the cellar.

The room was large for a root cellar, spanning at least half of the farmhouse. The stone walls of the foundation were unadorned here, giving the cellar a cavelike atmosphere. Along one side of the stone walls, Terry Harris had built a long row of rough pine shelves that held Mason jars full of pickles and preserves, half-empty boxes of onions and potatoes and at least a half a year's worth of commercially canned food.

"Benjy? Ronnie?" Her heart hammered a cadence of dread against her breastbone. "It's Miss Melissa. Are you in here?"

She listened over the rush of blood pulsing in her ears. At first, she heard nothing. But the softest of rustles in the back corner of the cellar drew her gaze in that direction.

"I heard that," Aaron murmured.

"Stay here," Melissa said quietly. She walked deeper into the cellar, toward a stack of large cardboard boxes that created a half wall between the door and the back of the cellar. Another rustling noise, louder than before, drew her around the boxes into the makeshift alcove.

Benjy and Ronnie huddled there, gazing at her with two pairs of fearful green eyes. Anxiety lined their little faces, making them look old beyond their years.

"Is Daddy still here?" the older one, Ronnie, whispered.

"Your daddy's gone away." She glanced at Aaron, who watched from his position at the bottom of the stairs.

"He'll be back," Ronnie said bleakly. "He always comes

back." He reached over and wrapped his thin arm around Benjy's narrow shoulders. "Mama said I should take care of Benjy. I did good, didn't I, Miss Melissa?"

Melissa blinked back hot tears. "You did great, Ronnie." She crouched beside them and took Ronnie's small hand. "I'm very proud of you. I bet your mama will be, too."

"Where's Mama?" Benjy whimpered. "I want Mama."

Melissa turned to look at Aaron again, but he wasn't there. She heard him climbing the stairs. What was he doing?

"Mama's upstairs. She needs to talk to some friends of hers for a few minutes, and then we can go see her." She wiped away the tears spilling from Benjy's eyes and pulled the little boy into her arms. "But I talked to her myself. She's okay. You don't have to worry about her."

"Daddy hits Mama." Shame reddened Ronnie's face.

"I know." Melissa stroked his cheek. "But he's not going to hit her anymore." Not if she had anything to say about it. And since he'd attacked her instead of Dinah this time, she'd have quite a bit to say about it.

She heard the door open upstairs and two sets of footsteps on the stairs. Pulling Benjy up on her hip, Melissa stood to see who was coming.

Aaron appeared first, followed by Dinah Harris. She'd combed her hair and washed her face sometime in the last few minutes, Melissa noted, and there was a bright if unconvincing smile pasted on her pale face.

"Mama!" Benjy wriggled frantically in Melissa's arms, and she let him go. He and Ronnie raced each other to their mother's waiting arms.

Melissa followed slowly, her gaze moving away from the heartbreaking reunion to level with Aaron's. He nodded for her to join him by the stairs.

"Quite a change," she murmured.

"I just reminded her she was still a mother," Aaron responded quietly.

Melissa wondered just how tough he'd been with Dinah to bring about her sudden change of demeanor. Aaron Cooper was apparently the kind of man who thought everybody could be bullied into doing his will, no matter how good his intentions might be. She'd known enough men like that to last her a lifetime.

She certainly didn't need another one.

Chapter Five

It took only a little coaxing, and a reminder that Terry Harris might get bail despite their best efforts, to convince Dinah that she and the children needed to go to a shelter for a few days. Melissa helped Dinah pack bags with a few days' worth of clothes for each of them. The shelter would provide the food and toiletries they'd need.

Outside, Aaron waited for them, standing with Riley Patterson and the red-haired deputy who'd lent Melissa her bulletproof vest. Aaron took the bags from Melissa and Dinah, looping both handles of the canvas bags over one large hand.

Melissa noted that the cruiser holding Terry Harris had already left the scene. She released a little sigh of relief, glad the boys didn't have to see their father in custody after everything else they'd already witnessed in their short lives.

"Mrs. Harris, this is Deputy Baker. She's going to drive you to the shelter. We've already called ahead to make sure there are rooms for you."

Dinah looked anxiously at Melissa. "I don't want to be separated from the boys."

"The rooms are right next to each other," Grace Baker told Dinah, her expression kind. "There's a door between them that you can leave open if you want. I asked for that special for you."

Dinah's look of surprise made Melissa's heart hurt. Had she so rarely seen kindness in her life that a little extra attention to her comfort was shocking to her?

She felt guilty that she hadn't probed deeper into Dinah's life, beyond the sketchy information the woman had given her once Melissa had signed on to be her pro bono attorney. She knew almost nothing about Dinah's life before her marriage. Had she been abused as a child, too? Had she seen marriage to Terry Harris as a way out of a miserable home situation?

Unfortunately, juggling her office duties and her pro bono work gave Melissa far too little time to dig more deeply into her clients' situations, beyond getting them out of danger and into a better situation.

Or maybe she didn't want to dig deeper. Maybe she was afraid looking too closely into her clients' lives would only stir up painful old memories she'd spent years overcoming.

Melissa watched Deputy Baker leading Dinah and the children to another cruiser. "I should go with her."

"I don't think you should," Aaron said.

"Why not? She's my client, for God's sake."

"You have a conflict of interest now," Riley Patterson said quietly. He gave her an apologetic look. "You're the complainant against Terry Harris in today's incident."

Melissa stared at him a moment, realization settling in. Of course she couldn't represent Dinah Harris now that she was pressing her own charges against Terry. It put an immediate strain on their client-attorney relationship.

"She needs an advocate with her," she said aloud. "I need to make a couple of calls." Melissa walked away from them, pulling out her phone. She managed to get through to one of the other pro bono lawyers on the Domestic Crisis Center's list and arranged for her to meet Dinah at the shelter. Then she headed for the cruiser, where Dinah and the boys sat in the back seat.

"Has something happened?" Dinah looked anxious.

"I have to turn your case over to another attorney, Dinah. I've arranged for Camille Dawkins to take over your advocacy."

"Because I set you up, right? To come here?" Dinah's face crumpled. "I'm sorry about that. I don't blame you for dumping me on somebody else after that."

"It's not that," Melissa assured her. "I'm going to press charges against Terry for assault. That makes working with you a conflict of interest, since you're a witness, and you're also still legally Terry's wife. I don't want to do anything to jeopardize the case against him."

Dinah licked her dry lips, a deep furrow lining the skin between her eyebrows. "I hate to think of my kids having to grow up with their daddy in prison."

"I know you do," Melissa said gently. "But the alternative is taking a beating every time he gets mad or drunk or high. He's not going to be able to talk me out of pressing charges or testifying against him, and you'll be completely out of the situation this way. You'll have had nothing to do with it. All you did was do what he asked by calling me here."

Tears spilled down Dinah's cheeks. "I'm so sorry for being so weak. I should never have made that call. I should have let him do whatever he was going to do to me, instead of you."

Melissa shook her head. "Blame Terry, not yourself. The only thing you owe me is to go to that shelter and get in a position to take care of yourself and your kids on your own. Promise me you're going to do that, okay?"

"I promise." Dinah's voice shook.

Melissa managed a smile, though she wasn't sure she believed Dinah's promise. She stepped back from the cruiser and closed the door, nodding to Deputy Baker.

As the cruiser drove away, Melissa walked slowly back to where Aaron now stood alone in the middle of the front lawn. He watched her approach, his eyes slightly narrowed. He said nothing, even when she was well within earshot. Something about his expression made her gut twist into a knot.

She broke the tense silence. "I'll meet you back at the Sheriff's Department to make a statement."

"You sure you're up to driving?"

"I'm fine to drive."

"You seem—jumpy."

So. He'd noticed her reaction to his attempts to handle her back in the house. What did he think, every woman in the world enjoyed being pawed by a big, self-important Neanderthal?

"I'm fine." She didn't bother to hide her irritation.

"Did I do something to piss you off?" he asked bluntly. "Because you're treating me like I'm radioactive."

"Just because I didn't want you to touch me?"

"Well, yeah."

"I don't have to explain my choices for my own body."

His brow furrowed. "You didn't worry about my choices for *my* body when you threw yourself at me earlier, did you?"

She felt a flutter of heat rise up her neck. "No. I'm sorry. I was a little stressed."

"I wasn't trying to do anything but give you support." His voice softened. "Is this about how I took Harris down earlier?"

She looked up to find him watching her, his expression so gentle that for a moment she wondered if she'd imagined the brute violence of his attack on Terry.

"I overstepped," he continued. "I know that. But he was trying to get to his gun to shoot you."

"I can't—" Her voice broke, forcing her to clear her throat and start over again. "I can't stand violence."

"Terry's the bad guy. I was trying to keep him from hurting you or anybody else again."

"You kept choking him when he was on the ground." A tremor ran through her belly. "You acted in anger, not protection."

When Aaron spoke, his voice was tight. "I was angry because he was trying to kill you. That's not the same thing as attacking him because he took my parking place."

She frowned at him, hating the way he was trying to make her feel unreasonable. "You could have killed him. No matter what he did, that's not acceptable."

"I already admitted I crossed a line."

"And that's it? You say you're sorry and everything's okay?" She shook her head, frustrated. "That's fine—until the next time your violent side gets the best of you."

Aaron's eyes narrowed. "Are we even having the same conversation?"

"Apparently not." She needed to get away from him. Now.

As she started to retreat to her car, Aaron reached out to stop her. He dropped his hand before he touched her, releasing a soft groan of frustration. "I don't have a violent side."

"You played football, Aaron. You probably go hunting. You carry a gun for a living, for God's sake." She sighed. "Of course you have a violent side."

"I played a game, Melissa. A game. I haven't hunted in years, and even then, my father taught me to kill only what I planned to eat." He stepped closer, his voice dropping lower. "And yes, I carry a gun. But I don't even pull it out of the holster unless I believe lives are in danger."

He made everything sound so reasonable, didn't he? He made her feel like an uptight priss who was completely over-reacting to the situation.

"We're not going to agree about this," she said.

"Clearly." He looked angry. *Typical,* she thought.

"I'm fine to drive," she added. "I'll meet you at the Sheriff's Department to give my formal statement."

"You're going to press charges, right?"

She lifted her chin. "Absolutely."

He surprised her by flashing a smile. "Good."

As she turned to walk to her car he fell into step, keeping a couple of feet's distance from her. He sped up as they got to the car, opening the driver's door for her.

She eyed him warily as she slid behind the wheel. "If you think you're going to change my mind about this by acting like a gentleman—"

"I don't think I'm going to change your mind at all," he said amiably. "But while you're driving to the station, maybe you should consider this. Whatever I did today, however violent you think it was, it probably saved your pretty little life."

He closed the door for her and headed across the lawn toward his own truck.

Melissa sat there, gripping the steering wheel tightly in her cold fingers. She tried to hold on to her anger, but the fire in her gut was fading fast.

Aaron Cooper called me pretty.

She was in so much trouble.

"On a scale of one to ten, with ten being the highest, how out of control was I with Harris?" Aaron asked Riley when they had a moment alone at the station later.

"Maybe a four. The guy was going for his gun, and you had an innocent civilian in the line of fire." Riley shrugged.

"I'd have been tempted to rip his head off myself, and you know I'm the soul of reason."

Aaron grinned. "Oh, yeah, I saw you when that creep went after Hannah. You were Mr. Calm, all right."

Riley returned the grin. "But I was in love with Hannah. What's your excuse, killer?"

Heat burned the back of Aaron's neck. He wasn't in love with Melissa Draper. He barely knew her, really.

But when he'd seen the bruises on her neck, all he could think about was making Harris pay for hurting her. She'd put her life on the line to help a woman who didn't know how to help herself. The world could use more people like her, and he'd be damned if he'd let a lowlife creep like Terry Harris lay another hand on her.

"Melissa Draper thinks you overreacted?" Riley asked.

"She thinks I have a violent streak."

Riley made a snorting noise. "You're a man. A little violence in your soul is a genetic trait."

"I'm pretty sure that's what Melissa thinks, too."

"I guess maybe she's seen a whole lot of that, if she's doing pro bono work for battered women." Riley grabbed the coffeepot and poured a cup. He tested it, grimacing. "God, this stuff is lethal." He took another drink.

Aaron poured a cup for himself. Riley was right. The coffee was strong enough to strip paint. Thank God.

"Are you interested in her?" Riley asked.

Aaron's hand gave a jerk at the unexpected question. Coffee sloshed over the side of his cup onto his desk. "Damn it!"

Riley handed him a paper napkin from a stash in his drawer. "It was a simple question."

Aaron mopped up the spilled coffee in silence. Riley had asked the wrong question. It didn't matter whether or not he liked Melissa. That was the easy part. Putting himself on the line for the long haul—that was the sticker.

When he had been younger, it had been easier just to play the field. Nobody had expected him to settle down, even the girls he dated. But the older he got, the more he could feel the weight of expectations. *You're pushing thirty, Aaron. Why aren't you married yet?*

Because love didn't last forever, that's why. Because even when you thought you'd found the one, you could still end up in a messy divorce like his brother Sam or standing over a woman's grave like J.D., or, hell, sticking a gun barrel in your mouth and pulling the trigger the way his college roommate Ricky Long had done when the girl he'd asked to marry him said *no.*

Love was dangerous.

"Hey, Aaron, Ms. Draper's here to see you." Blake Clayton entered the bullpen, Melissa right behind him. She didn't look quite as annoyed as she had when he'd left her, he was relieved to see. Maybe she'd given thought to what he'd told her.

"Have a seat." He waved her toward the steel and vinyl chair beside his desk and took his seat behind it.

"First, I have something to say."

He looked at her warily. "Yes?"

"Thank you. You did save my life today, and it was wrong of me not to say something before now."

Her prim recitation almost made him smile. He resisted the urge, knowing she'd probably think he was making fun of her. She could be touchy.

He couldn't blame her for it, though. Maybe he didn't remember her from high school as well as either of them might have liked, but he remembered well enough how the group of friends he'd run around with treated people like Melissa and her friends. Not exactly one of his fondest memories of Chickasaw County High School.

At least she'd gotten the last laugh. She was a lawyer now, living in a big—if fire-damaged—house on the moneyed end of Tuckahaw Road, while until only a couple of months ago, he'd still been living in the run-down two-bedroom bungalow he'd been renting since just after college. Until his recent promotion, he'd been taking all the extra hours he could at the cop shop, not to mention volunteering for a dangerous DEA joint operation, just to make sure the bills were paid on time.

"So, I guess I need to give you my statement," she said.

"Deputy Patterson's going to handle that."

Melissa looked over at Riley, who smiled at her. She looked back at Aaron. "Is this because of what I said before?"

He shook his head. "I just need to interview Harris as soon as they finish booking him. I'm wondering if he has an alibi for last night when someone set fire to your house."

"Good luck with that. His lawyer's already here. She was out in the hall before I came in," Melissa said. "Sometimes I think she monitors the police radio."

"She?"

"Tina Lewis with the Betancourt firm. She's tough. You're not going to have an easy time with her."

There went his dinner plans. But, to his surprise, the thought came as a relief, not a disappointment. Yet another go-nowhere dinner date with a beautiful but emotionally distant woman didn't hold much appeal anymore.

The woman herself entered the bullpen, dressed in a neatly tailored suit that hugged rather than hid her curves. She was tall, blonde and well-built, more striking than beautiful. In the dozens of times she and Aaron had crossed paths over the last couple of years, he'd admired her dynamic energy and her razor-sharp wit. They'd been out together once before, and the evening had gone well though it hadn't led to anything more than a quick kiss goodnight.

Then Aaron had gone on temporary assignment with the DEA and hadn't really given her much more thought until this morning, when he'd been looking for something to distract him from how much Melissa Draper was starting to get under his skin.

He glanced at Melissa and found her watching him, her expression shuttered. He wished he knew what she was thinking. He was certain he'd find her less intriguing if she weren't such a mystery.

"I guess you realize our date tonight is off," Tina said when she reached his desk. She glanced at Melissa. "Hello, Melissa. Is one of your clients here as well?"

"Not today." Melissa's eyes narrowed as she looked from Tina to Aaron. "Actually, I'm here to give a statement against your client."

Tina's smile faded as she took in Melissa's disheveled appearance and the bruises on her throat. "You'll understand if we end our conversation here, then?"

"Of course." Melissa shot a considering look at Aaron as she stood and crossed to Riley's desk.

Aaron watched Riley start taking her statement. Her tension was back.

"Did I interrupt something besides business?" Tina asked in a low voice, dropping into the seat Melissa had just vacated.

Aaron forced his attention back to Tina. "I'm investigating her case."

"Her unfortunate run-in with my client?"

"You mean his brutal attack on an unarmed woman he had his battered wife lure to their house with a phone call?" Aaron grimaced. "No, not that one. Unless your client also tried to burn down her house last night with her in it."

"She has plenty of enemies besides Mr. Harris," Tina said firmly. "Is there evidence linking my client to the fire?"

It would take days, even weeks, for the state crime lab to process everything. An arson attempt that hadn't resulted in injuries or major property damage wouldn't be high on their list of priorities. So he ignored her question. "By enemies, I assume you mean other wife beaters?"

"Alleged wife beaters," Tina corrected with an upward twitch of one eyebrow. "And yes. Among others."

"What others?"

"You'll have to take that up with Melissa." She stood. "Now, will you kindly arrange for me to see my client?"

Aaron glanced over at Riley and saw that Melissa was standing as well, apparently through giving her statement. He looked back at Tina. "Tell you what, Tina—Riley Patterson's in charge of the assault case. He's right over there." Aaron pointed toward his brother-in-law.

Tina's brow furrowed. "Aaron, why exactly did you ask me out to dinner, out of the blue, after all these months?"

"Just had a night free and thought we could catch up."

"You just picked up an arson case overnight and you have a night free?" Tina appeared unconvinced.

He didn't answer, because the truth would only make her angry. "Better catch Riley while he's available."

The look she gave him could have corroded metal, but she headed for Riley's desk without further delay, nodding to Melissa as they passed in the middle of the bullpen.

Melissa barely glanced Aaron's way before heading for the exit. Rounding his desk quickly, he hurried to catch up with her. He opened the bullpen door to let her through. "You heading back to the lake?"

"Your sister is probably sick of my dog by now."

He fell into step as she continued down the hallway. "Tina

said you have enemies besides the husbands and boyfriends of the women you represent. What did she mean?"

Melissa shrugged. "Ask your girlfriend."

He frowned. "She said to ask you. And she's not my girlfriend. I don't really do the girlfriend thing, you know?"

Melissa's eyes narrowed. Aaron realized his words must have sounded like a warning.

Had he meant them to be?

Melissa paused at the exit door. "Know what I think? I think it's likely Terry Harris set the fire at my house. And when it didn't work, he had his wife lure me to their place so he could finish the job. So maybe you should do what you said—look into his alibi and stop worrying so much about me and my other alleged enemies."

He watched her leave through the sheriff department's glass front door. She walked with her back stiff and her eyes straight forward, but he could tell she knew he was watching her. It made her nervous as hell.

Why don't you want me to look more closely at your house fire, Melissa? What else do you have to hide?

Chapter Six

Melissa had thought Aaron might show up at the guest cottage doorstep before nightfall, but he didn't. Instead she'd spent the rest of the night trying to convince herself that it had been Terry Harris who had tried to burn down her house. He'd had motive. He'd had the means—all he'd have needed was a matchbook and the gasoline she stored in her shed. And the deputies would figure out sooner or later if he'd had the opportunity.

Meanwhile, she couldn't keep living life as if she were in the cross hairs of a killer. She'd already missed a day of work. She might not have any cases on the court docket for the next week, but she could still find ways to be useful at the office.

Anything was better than sitting around the Cooper family's guest cabin, mooning over Aaron Cooper.

She had been a little disconcerted to realize just how quickly her anger at him had faded once she'd had time to calm down in private. Beyond what he'd done to Terry that afternoon, he hadn't shown much evidence of violent behavior, she had to admit. He was a little free with the touching, but not everyone found that kind of behavior as threatening as she did.

Not everyone shared her experiences with men who had bad tempers and no self-control.

And it meant something that she'd flung herself into his arms that afternoon. Something that had nothing to do with hormones or lingering teenage fantasies.

In that moment, she'd felt safe. Safe and protected.

So maybe Aaron Cooper wasn't really a violent brute. But she couldn't let herself start thinking of him as someone she could trust. She had to get her mind off him, off her crazy situation, and do something constructive.

She decided to leave Jasper with Amy DeLong, a friend from high school who worked from home and had started dog-sitting Jasper on weekdays while Melissa was at work. She couldn't bear leaving him in a small kennel during the day, and he was too young and rambunctious yet to leave alone for long periods of time while she was gone.

Amy greeted her at the door, a newspaper tucked under one arm. Her eyes widened at the sight of Melissa. "Thank God. Are you okay?"

Melissa frowned. "I'm fine. Why?"

Amy pulled the newspaper from under her arm and waved it at Melissa. "I can't decide if you're a hero or a crazy idiot."

Melissa caught the newspaper on Amy's last wave and held it still enough to read the headline at the top of the local daily. "Chickasaw County man charged with assault." A mug shot of Terry Harris sat below the headline.

"I didn't get a paper this morning," she said calmly. "The article made me sound crazy?"

"Some deputy was quoted saying you drew the guy out of a hostage standoff." Amy took the paper back and scanned the columns, finally punching her finger at one near the middle. "There."

A deputy? Surely not Aaron. He'd know that she'd prefer her privacy, wouldn't he?

It hadn't been Aaron, she saw when she took the paper

back from Amy. The article quoted Blake Clayton, who'd made her sound like a combination of Joan of Arc and Buffy the Vampire Slayer. Though she normally hated even the thought of violence, in this case she thought she might be justified in hunting Blake Clayton down and throttling him.

At least her law office was located in a bigger city in a different county. It wasn't likely the Borland paper had picked up the story.

But as it turned out, Borland apparently wasn't as big or distant as she'd hoped. When she walked in she found almost everyone in the office huddled around Donna the receptionist, reading the morning newspaper over Donna's shoulder.

Dalton Brant was the first to look up and see her. "Hail the conquering heroine," he said, his voice tinted with thinly veiled hostility. She wasn't his favorite person around the office these days. He thought her last promotion had been at his expense.

Vicki Trammell's reaction, on the other hand, was to hurry to her side and give her a hug. "Do you think he's the one who set the fire?" She walked Melissa over to the break area, where a pot of coffee sat steaming on a small hot plate. "He had to be, don't you think?"

Melissa took the cup of coffee Vicki poured, the hot stoneware warm against her cold fingers. "It's likely."

Carter Morgan emerged from his office, his gaze seeking her out. With a gesture of his head for her to join him, he retreated to his office.

"I have to talk to Carter." Melissa handed the cup of coffee back to Vicki.

"Close the door and have a seat," Carter said when she reached the open doorway of his office.

She did as he asked, settling into the comfortable armchair across from his wide mahogany desk. "I know you said I could take the rest of the week off—"

"You're not in trouble," he said gently. "But I still think you should take the rest of the week off. Now more than ever." He tapped his hand on the folded newspaper sitting by his desk blotter.

"May I?" She gestured toward the newspaper.

He handed it over. She unfolded it, scanning for the article. It wasn't under the banner, as it had been in the Chickasaw County paper, but the article had made the front page, below the fold.

They'd picked up Blake Clayton's quote, she saw with her heart sinking. "It wasn't as dramatic as this suggests."

"You'll never be able to convince anyone of that. I'm afraid you'll just have to wait out the notoriety." Carter flashed her a rueful smile. "I don't fault you, of course, for what you did. I admire your courage. I've always thought highly of you for your work with domestic abuse victims. You know that."

"But?"

"But our clients expect a certain amount of discretion from the people who represent them."

Melissa frowned. "You think I've been indiscreet?"

"Not intentionally. But I think you should take a few days off as I suggested."

"Sir—"

"Don't look at it as punishment. You haven't had a full week off the entire time you've worked for this firm."

"I like to work," she said defensively.

"And I like that you like to work." Carter laughed softly. "But everyone needs time off. And this is a very good time for you to take advantage of your light court schedule."

"Because I'm notorious?" she asked tartly.

His quick look warned her she was getting close to crossing a line. But his voice was gentle when he spoke. "Can you please do as I ask, Melissa, without debating me to death? Just this once?"

"But you're still shorthanded, with Alice out." Alice had left for vacation the Friday before and wouldn't be back until the following week, leaving Vicki as the office's only clerical assistant. Everyone in the office had been doing some of their own grunt work to take up the slack. "If I take next week off, everyone will have to work that much harder to keep up."

"We'll manage." Carter stood, signaling the end of the conversation. Clearly, he wasn't going to listen to her arguments.

She rose, tamping down a sense of embarrassment. Even though she knew she'd only done what had had to be done the day before, she felt as if she'd somehow disappointed her boss, the last thing she'd ever want to do. Carter had offered her a job right out of law school as his personal assistant until she passed the bar. Then, even though he hadn't had any openings for litigators at that time, he'd gone out of his way to create a position for her, mentoring her with patience and professionalism.

She owed her career to him, and now, however unintentionally, she'd let him down. She couldn't bear to let people down.

"I'm sorry," she said as he walked her to the door.

"You did nothing wrong. It's just the way of things." He patted her shoulder. "You said you're staying on Gossamer Lake?"

Out of the corner of her eye, she saw that her colleagues still gathered in the front office were looking her way, curious about what Carter had wanted to talk to her about in private.

Feeling self-conscious, she nodded. "It's at Cooper Cove Marina. A friend's parents own the place. I'm staying at their guest cottage, at least through this weekend." She hoped to find another place before long, not wanting to impose on the Coopers any more than necessary.

"Perfect. Could you deliver an affidavit for me to the Betancourt firm over in Maybridge? I know it's a little out of the way—"

"No problem," she said. "I'll be happy to."

"I left it with Vicki to deliver, but Charles needs her to take notes at a client meeting before she can go. This solves the problem of getting the file to Betancourt before lunch time, when I told them I'd have it there."

She felt the curious eyes of her coworkers on her as she headed for the exit. "I'm taking the rest of this week off," she said aloud, getting it over with.

"With Alice off, too?" Dalton grumbled.

"Don't listen to him," Vicki murmured, nudging her away from Dalton. "He's just jealous because he's never been on the front page of the *Borland Courier*."

"Nothing to be jealous of," Melissa assured her quietly. "Listen, Carter asked me to deliver that affidavit he left with you, the one going to Betancourt."

"Oh, okay." Vicki went to her desk and pulled a sealed manila envelope from one of her desk drawers. "Here you go. It goes to Tina Lewis."

Great, Melissa thought. Just what she was hoping for, another run-in with Tina Lewis. She walked with Vicki to the exit. "I'll check in now and then to see if y'all need anything. And call me if anything comes up with any of my cases."

"Of course." Vicki opened the door for her. She flashed Melissa a rueful grin. "Try to stay out of trouble, okay?"

Melissa smiled back. "I'll do my best."

Traffic was light and she made decent time on the drive to Maybridge. She'd hoped she'd be able to drop off the files and be on her way, but considering her luck over the last couple of days, she should've known better. Tina Lewis was standing in the foyer of the pretty, old brick colonial two-story that housed the Betancourt Law Office when Melissa entered.

Tina's eyebrows lifted. "Long time no see."

"I'm playing errand girl today," Melissa replied, holding out the envelope. "From Carter Morgan."

"Thanks." Tina took the envelope and handed it to the dark-haired receptionist at the front desk. "Please have my assistant take care of that. She's been waiting for it."

"See you around," Melissa said, turning to leave.

Tina caught up with her at the door. "I'll walk you out."

Melissa slanted a look at her, surprised. She and Tina Lewis had never been particularly cordial, thanks to their frequent clashes in court.

"Headed back to work?" Tina asked.

"Actually, no. I'm apparently a bit too high profile at the moment. I'm taking a few days off until the furor dies down."

"The news account *was* a bit overwrought."

"No argument from me." Melissa stopped by her car. "I guess I should be going."

"I heard the fire made a mess of your house," Tina said. "Surely you're not staying there."

Melissa could tell her question wasn't just idle curiosity. "I'm staying at a friend's place for a few days."

"Aaron's?"

Ah, they'd reached the real point of Tina's show of cordiality. "I'm not supposed to tell people where I'm staying."

"He seems very interested in you."

"He's investigating the fire."

Tina smiled. "You know, Melissa, I admire you. I know I don't show it much because we're always across the table from each other in court, but I do respect your passion and your skill. So I'm going to give you some advice."

"About what?" Melissa asked warily.

"About Aaron Cooper." Tina pushed a loose strand of

blond hair out of her eyes. "He's not a forever kind of guy, you know? I don't know if he ever will be."

"And that's okay with you?"

"Well, yeah. No strings works great for me, at least for now. And if that's your thing, then great. I'm not out here staking a claim. I just get the feeling that you're the type of woman who'd want more from a man. I've seen people burned by guys like Aaron before. I thought you should know what you're dealing with."

Melissa couldn't decide whether to be annoyed by Tina's presumption or grateful for the warning. Not that it made any difference. She wasn't looking for a relationship any more than Tina was, even if her reasons were different.

"Thank you," she said finally, deciding to go with gratitude. "But you're worrying for nothing. I'm not interested in a relationship, and as you say, neither is Aaron."

"Well, good." Tina stepped back so Melissa could open the driver's door of the Volkswagen. "Take care."

Melissa tried not to think about Tina's warning on the drive to the lake. Her surroundings offered a measure of distraction; the road from Maybridge to Gossamer Ridge was one of the more scenic in the county, skimming one of the mountain ridges part of the way and affording travelers a breathtaking view of Gossamer Lake glimmering like a jewel in the clear morning air as it reflected the cloudless azure sky.

It was also a nightmare for someone as afraid of heights as Melissa was.

Though most people would have been enchanted by her surroundings, Melissa could barely breathe as she navigated the sharp curves of the mountain road, trying not to look at the steep drop-offs that seemed only inches away from the narrow shoulder and were separated from the road by a flimsy-looking aluminum guard rail.

She didn't relax again until she passed the turnoff to Crybaby Falls and headed onto the gentle downhill incline toward Cooper Cove Marina. The treacherous bluffs that had been her nightmarish companion for the last few miles leveled off as the road itself moved downward toward the valley and lake below. Piney forest surrounded her on either side, the sun just beginning to crest the trees to the east casting long, spiky shadows across the road ahead.

Suddenly Melissa heard an odd cracking sound. A split second later her car gave a violent lurch to one side.

She tightened her grip on the wheel, pulling the Volkswagen back toward her lane but the small car fought her effort at control. A sickening *whump-whump* noise told her what had happened. One of her tires had blown.

She eased the Volkswagen to a stop and cut the engine, her heart going a mile a minute. If the tire had blown a few minutes ago, while she had been driving along that steep drop-off—

She heard another soft crack, and felt something thunk against her car. The blow felt pretty substantial, too hard to be an acorn falling or a loose rock pinging down from the side of the mountain. She opened her door and started to get out when the same cracking sound happened a third time. Almost instantaneously, the glass in the back driver's-side window shattered.

She turned to look at the broken window, her mind sluggish. But at the sight of the spider web of cracks radiating around a small hole left in the safety glass, adrenaline exploded into her system nearly knocking her off her feet.

Someone was shooting at her.

Diving into the front seat, Melissa crouched low and scrambled for her purse, which had fallen into the floorboard. Outside the morning had gone silent, or was it just that the pulse roaring in her ears drowned out everything else? She finally found her purse and pulled her cell phone from the outside pocket.

She had to get out of here. Even if it was just some hunter with bad aim, shooting at anything that moved out there, all the more reason to get the hell out of his line of fire.

Driving with the flat wouldn't be easy, and it would probably ruin her rims, but it was better than taking a bullet to the head.

She stayed hunched over as she pulled herself back into the driver's seat and restarted the engine. The steering wheel felt unwieldy, and the car shook and shimmied as she pulled back onto the road with the flattened tire. Suddenly the road to the lake looked impossibly long and winding.

Her heart pounding, she glanced at the cell phone still clutched in her right hand. *Aaron. Call Aaron.*

She found herself punching in his number, which she'd programmed into her phone the day before.

He answered on the second ring. "Cooper."

"Aaron, it's Melissa. I think someone just shot at me."

AARON'S BODY went cold at Melissa's soft words. "What?"

Her voice seemed distant, hard to hear over the sound of a car engine and an odd thumping sound on her end of the line. "I think someone shot at me. My tire blew, and when I stopped, something hit my car hard. I got out to look and my back window shattered."

Son of a bitch. He knew he shouldn't have let her walk away without a guard. "Where are you?"

"Driving down Ridge Road, toward the lake. I'm about three miles from your folks' place."

"Are you still hearing shots?"

"No."

Thank God for that. "Okay, go straight to the marina. I don't care if you start seeing sparks from the tire rims, just keep going. Go to the bait shop and tell my folks everything. Wait for me there, okay?"

"Okay." She sounded relieved.

He hung up and grabbed his jacket.

Riley looked up from his desk. "What's happened?"

Aaron told him. "I'm heading to the marina."

"Want me to come with you?"

Aaron managed a tense grin. "You just want to see Hannah."

"You say that like it's a bad thing."

They took Aaron's truck. About halfway to the marina, Aaron put his cell phone on speaker and dialed the number to the marina bait shop. His mother answered.

"Hey, Mom. Has Melissa Draper gotten there yet?"

"She's right here," Beth Cooper answered.

After a brief pause, Melissa came on the line. Her voice trembled a little. "Your dad's outside looking at the car. He thinks they're definitely bullet holes."

"Did you see anyone around you? Was there other traffic on the road?"

"Not that time of day," she answered. "I was the only one on Ridge Road, and I didn't see anyone in the woods but it happened so fast."

"How far did you go after your tire blew out?"

"I'm not sure. Maybe a hundred yards? I wasn't going that fast, and I stopped almost immediately."

Turning off the main highway, Aaron headed the truck down the access road to the marina, going faster than he should. He saw Riley slant a curious look his way as the truck's tires squealed on a sharp curve.

He slowed his speed a bit, as the road to the lake was full of twists and sharp turns. "Did you hear anything that could have been a gunshot?"

"I'm not sure. I thought I heard something each time, like

a cracking sound. But it wasn't what I thought a gunshot would sound like."

Aaron smiled slightly. "Have you ever heard a gunshot? Not counting television."

"No," Melissa admitted.

Cooper Cove Marina came into sight around one final turn. Aaron pulled into the small parking lot in front of the bait shop, spotting his father and his brother J.D. examining Melissa's little white Volkswagen. They looked up when he and Riley stepped out of the truck.

"I'm thinking a .22 rifle," J.D. pronounced as Aaron joined him next to the shredded left back tire. "It had to have come from some distance or she'd have seen whoever had been shooting."

"Unless he was camouflaged," Riley pointed out.

Aaron frowned. "This is crazy. Why would a woman like Melissa Draper be on somebody's hit list? She's nobody."

J.D. cleared his throat, his gaze shifting to a point behind Aaron. Aaron turned around to find Melissa standing a couple of feet away, her arms hugging herself as if she were cold. Her pale blue eyes met Aaron's in an unwavering gaze, though he thought he saw a hint of hurt behind her half smile.

"You're right. I'm not the sort of person people want to kill," she said aloud. "But here we are anyway."

He crossed to her, lifting his hand to squeeze her arm but pausing when he remembered how she'd reacted to his unwanted touches the day before. He dropped his hand to his side. "Are you okay?"

Her gaze dropped with his hand. "Just freaked-out more than anything."

"Let's get you inside." The place was surrounded by woods on three sides, with the open lake in front of them. If someone wanted Melissa dead, it wouldn't be hard to take another potshot at her standing out here in the open.

In the bait shop, his mother was waiting on a fishing customer. Aaron eyed the man as he gathered up his purchases and headed outside.

"Do you know that guy?" he asked his mother.

"Ray Pelham. Comes by for night crawlers every couple of days," Beth answered.

"Navy Lieutenant J. G. Pelham, retired. Good guy." J.D. clapped Aaron's back. "Not everybody's the enemy, Aaron."

Aaron turned to Riley. "Handle the evidence retrieval from the vehicle. We're also going to need to take a look at the woods near where the shooting occurred, see if the bastard left any shell casings around."

Riley nodded and headed back outside.

Aaron turned back to Melissa, lowering his voice. "You've clearly made an enemy. A determined one, from the looks of it. You don't need to wander around Chickasaw County alone while this creep's still at large."

She gave him a worried look. "What are you saying?"

"I've got vacation time accrued. Maybe it's a good time to take it. Because you need around-the-clock protection."

Chapter Seven

Melissa shivered inside the cab of Aaron's truck, staring out at the woods where Riley Patterson and four other deputies were searching for signs of expended rifle cartridges. Aaron remained in the driver's seat next to her, listening in to the chatter on the other deputies' radios.

Still trying to play bodyguard, she thought.

"Wouldn't you rather be out there helping with the search?"

He shook his head. "I'm fine right here."

"We don't even know this was an actual attempt on my life," she protested. "This is still hunting season, right?"

"Yeah. Deer season's over at the end of January."

"So there are bound to be hunters around here, right?"

"It wasn't a hunter who shot at you, Melissa."

"You can't know that."

"If it had just been the tire, sure. Maybe it could be a hunter. But the guy shot at you a good hundred yards past that first shot. That's intentional."

She dropped her gaze. "I don't know how this is happening. Terry Harris is in jail, and I don't really know who else—"

"Don't you have other domestic abuse clients?"

"A few. None of their abusers are as volatile as Terry, and none has threatened me in particular."

"I still need the list of names, so I can look into their whereabouts this morning and the night of the fire."

She met his gaze firmly. "No."

"No?"

"Attorney-client privilege."

"Then ask their permission."

"No. My clients have been through hell, and most of them are finally getting their lives back to some semblance of peace and order. I am not going to involve them in a police investigation that drags their abusers back into their lives."

Aaron growled with frustration. "What am I supposed to do, then? How am I supposed to protect you if I have no idea who's trying to hurt you?"

"I can check into their whereabouts on my own," she suggested. "I have contact with some of their probation officers. I know some of their families. I can make some inquiries about their recent activities."

"And if you find a suspect? Aren't you still bound by your confidentiality rules?" Aaron asked.

"Look, how about this—if any of the men in question seem viable as suspects, I'll ask their victims for permission to share the information with you."

He didn't look happy with her proposed solution, but he didn't argue the point. "Is there anybody else?" he asked. "Besides disgruntled wife beaters? Any contentious cases you've handled through your law firm?"

"Contract law doesn't usually inspire murderous passions."

"What about personally? Are you seeing anyone? Maybe just broke up with someone?"

"No. I haven't been seeing anyone for a while." Not since Evan Hallman.

He gave her a skeptical look. "How long is a while?"

She wasn't about to admit it had been four years. He

probably found her pathetic enough as it was. "It's not an ex-boyfriend. Trust me." Certainly not Evan, who was still locked up in a North Carolina prison.

"How about the people you work with? Do any of them know where you're staying since the fire?"

"I guess they all do, since I told Carter where he could reach me right in front of them all." She sighed. "But it can't be anyone at the office, Aaron. I'm not into workplace drama. I don't backstab. I don't sleep my way around the place. I don't have a cushy corner office someone covets—" She stopped short, because that wasn't entirely true. Not the corner office part, but there was someone at work who was a little jealous of her, wasn't there?

Dalton Brant wasn't her biggest fan.

But the idea of Dalton picking up a cap gun, much less a hunting rifle, was so ludicrous she almost laughed aloud. "There's a guy at the office who thinks I leapfrogged over him for my last promotion, but honestly, it wasn't enough of a promotion to inspire murder. He just takes joy in snarking at me at the office."

"You'd be surprised how little it takes to enrage some people," Aaron said.

She gave him a pointed look. "I defend abused spouses. There's little that surprises me anymore."

"Tell me about this guy. What's his name?"

"I'm not going to narc on someone I work with."

"It's not narcing, Melissa. Someone has tried to kill you. Twice. I'm trying to make sure there's not a third attempt, but you're making it hard for me to do my job."

"I don't mean to."

His brow furrowed. "I'm beginning to wonder if that's true. You aren't exactly a charter member of the Aaron Cooper fan club, are you?"

On the contrary, she thought. *I probably started the*

damned thing. "Whatever you think I think of you, I'm certainly not trying to thwart your investigation."

"Then tell me the name of the man at work."

She sighed, knowing he had to at least look into any possible lead. "Dalton Brant. But he's not the guy, Aaron."

"We'll see."

She grabbed his arm. He looked down at her hand, then slowly back up at her. The temperature in the truck cab rose at least ten degrees, sending heat flushing into her cheeks. She withdrew her hand, but the feel of his rough denim jacket lingered on her fingertips, shooting a tingle up her arm.

She cleared her throat. "Don't harass Dalton, okay? Can't you just ask around without confronting him directly?"

"Are you afraid of him?"

She stared at him, appalled. "No, of course not."

"Then why do you care if I ask him a few questions?"

She looked down at her hands. "I don't want to create a big stir at work, okay? I like my job."

"You think your boss would fire you just because you're a victim of a murder attempt?"

"I'm not a victim," she said bluntly. She'd spent the last four years making sure she never would be again.

"Okay." He fell silent. The truck cab seemed impossibly small all of a sudden.

The crackle of the police radio made her jump. She smiled self-consciously while Aaron listened to the dispatch call for a patrol car to respond to a traffic accident on the other side of the county. "I feel like I'm keeping you from your job," she said when he turned to look at her.

"This is my job." He tapped his thumbs on the steering wheel, his brow creased in thought. "You said your whole office heard you tell your boss where you were staying, right?"

"Right."

"Did you come straight here from the office?"

"No, Carter asked me to drop off some papers to another law firm over in Maybridge."

"Maybridge? That's at least twenty miles out of the way."

"Still sort of on the way here," she said, not sure she was following his line of thought. "I didn't mind."

"Who knew you were going to Maybridge before coming here?"

"Well, Carter, of course. And Vicki Trammell—she was supposed to take the papers, but since I was heading this way Carter asked me to take them instead and save her the trip."

Suddenly, she understood his questions.

She stared at him in horror. "You think someone from my office shot at me."

AARON GAUGED her reaction, wondering if she'd been soft selling Dalton Brant's antipathy for her. But she looked utterly flummoxed.

"You don't think it's even remotely possible?" he asked.

She shook her head. "Of course not."

"Are Carter Morgan and Vicki Trammell the only people who knew you'd be detouring to Maybridge?"

"I told Vicki what Carter asked me to do, and everybody else in the office was right there. Any one of them could have overheard. It's a small office."

Aaron released a long, slow breath. So much for trimming the suspect list. "How many people work in your office?"

"Eight. Carter, of course. His partner Charles Dailey. Dalton. Vicki. Kent Long, our go-to guy on bankruptcy law. Gregory Champion—Carter's been looking at making him a partner, so he's hardly in the frame of mind to off a junior associate," she added with barely veiled sarcasm. "Alice Gaines, but she's on vacation this week. And me."

Aaron caught a hint of hesitation in her voice when she mentioned Alice Gaines. "Tell me about Alice."

Melissa's brow furrowed. "Why? I told you she was on vacation this week."

"Is she another lawyer?"

"No, she's a paralegal like Vicki, only Vicki works mainly with Carter and Charles. Alice helps the rest of us more."

There was still a hint of uncertainty in her voice when she spoke about Alice. Aaron made a mental note to ask more questions about the vacationing paralegal.

"Nobody at my office would kill me. Nobody at my office has any reason to try to kill me," Melissa insisted. "Yes, Dalton Brant can be a jerk, but he's also a very smart guy. He knows he might be a suspect. He's not stupid enough to risk his freedom over a promotion."

"Probably not," Aaron agreed. And if the timing of this latest ambush wasn't so intriguing, her coworkers would probably be well down the list of possible suspects. But how else could someone have known that Melissa would be driving down Ridge Road at this particular time?

Melissa's voice grew more plaintive. "Please promise me you're not going to harass my coworkers about this. I don't want them to know this is happening to me."

He cocked his head to one side, looking at her through slightly narrowed eyes. She seemed genuinely mortified by the thought. "Why not? They might want to help you."

She didn't answer, though a faint flush rose in her cheeks. An almost pained look flashed across her face before she tamped it down and looked away.

He decided not to push her. Maybe if he backed off the intensity, she might relax and open up a bit more. He searched his mind for a safer topic, one that might allow her to let down her guard. "How did you get into the pro bono stuff you do?"

Apparently he'd chosen the exact wrong topic. Her spine stiffened, and she kept her expression carefully neutral when she answered. "I volunteered with a domestic abuse hotline for a while during my last year of law school. It affected me a lot. So when I got the chance to help women abused by people they loved, I knew I had to do it."

"A lot of people wouldn't have wanted to get involved." Aaron was impressed by her courage. Domestic violence situations were messy and dangerous. "Can't be an easy job."

"What about your job?" She sounded eager to change the subject. "Being a deputy can't be easy, either. What made you decide to choose that line of work?"

"Your dad, believe it or not." He grinned. "Remember when Seth Becker and I rolled Cliff Mulligan's yard after the state championship my senior year?" The sheer volume of toilet paper streams they'd left in the Mulligans' front yard had been the stuff of legends. Aaron had used three weeks worth of savings from his grocery sacking job to pay for the toilet paper.

He looked at her expectantly, hoping his foray into their shared past combined with the mention of her father might at least make her smile. But if anything, her expression shuttered further. "No, I don't remember that."

He looked surprised. "Really? Thirty rolls of toilet paper hanging from the Mulligans' big old oak tree?"

She shook her head.

"Come on! It was all over school the next Monday, because your dad hauled us in and talked our parents into letting us stay overnight at the county lockup to teach us a lesson."

Her brow furrowed prettily as if she were genuinely trying to remember. Finally, a glimmer of recognition shone in her blue eyes. "Oh. That was in December, right? My mom had an accident around that time, and my dad arranged for me to be out of school for a couple of weeks to take care of her."

"Oh." Now that he thought of it, part of Deputy Draper's harangue against him and Seth that night had included his irritation at being dragged away from his injured wife to deal with a couple of idiot hooligans. Or something like that. "I'm sorry. I hope she was okay."

"Just broke her arm, but she couldn't do a lot of stuff for herself for a while." Looking away from him, Melissa cleared her throat. "How did a night in jail make you want to be a cop? I mean, you went to college on a football scholarship, and all I ever heard about you was how you were going to be the top NFL draft pick. Wasn't that your real dream?"

Aaron's mood darkened immediately. It had been almost seven years since a late hit had torn his anterior cruciate ligament and ended his dream of being an NFL star, but the memory of what fate had torn from him still had the power to wound. "It didn't make me want to be a cop right away," he answered, forcing his mind away from a future he'd never have. "I spent most of my college years with stars in my eyes and a lot of voices in my ears telling me I was going to be a millionaire pro player."

"But that didn't work out." Melissa looked up at him, her expression sympathetic.

"No, it didn't." He sighed. "So when I had to think of something else to do with my life, I remembered how your dad's tough love act made me take a long, hard look at how I was behaving back then. I wanted to be different. Your dad helped me grow up a lot that night."

"Tough love," Melissa echoed softly, turning her gaze away from Aaron and staring down the road ahead.

He followed her gaze and saw Gossamer Lake glimmering like a sapphire in the midday sun. A surge of emotion rippled through him, a sense of belonging.

Gossamer Lake was home.

If he'd lived the pro ball dream, how often would he have been able to come back home to Chickasaw County to visit? Once or twice a year? How much more isolated would he have become?

Here, at least, he had his family. God love them, they'd never turn their backs on him.

"Did you ever tell my father he changed your life?" Melissa's voice sounded strange. Constrained.

"He'd already retired by the time I graduated from college and came back here. I guess maybe he'd had enough of dealing with self-absorbed little jerks like me."

She finally turned and looked at him again. "Do you like being a deputy? Even if it's not your first dream?"

"Yeah, I do," he admitted with a smile, meaning it.

Her smile in response looked strained. "Even if it means putting up with self-absorbed little jerks like you once were?"

He chuckled. "Even that. I don't do as much of that now that I'm an investigator, though." He rubbed his hands together, blowing on them. The cold outside had begun to overwhelm the lingering heat in the cab's interior. "It's cold out here. Maybe I should take you back to the house. If I know my mom, she's probably got a big crock pot of chili cooking for lunch. Maybe we could mooch a little from her."

She blinked, and he thought for a moment he saw moisture clinging to her eyelashes. But when she looked at him again, she was clear-eyed. "I don't want to impose on your mom."

He almost laughed. His mother lived for the chance to be hospitable. It was her most endearing—and exasperating—trait. "Trust me, she makes extra because she counts on at least one or two of us kids showing up to mooch," Aaron assured her.

"And bring tag-along friends, too?" She gave him a skeptical look.

"Absolutely." He radioed Riley to tell him they were heading back to the lake on a lunch break.

"Tell your mom to save some for me," Riley radioed back.

"See?" Aaron cranked the truck. "Why do you think so many of us still live nearby?"

Once again, he saw a strange melancholy light in her blue eyes for just a second.

Then her expression shuttered again.

"I KNOW it's short notice, but I haven't taken any of my vacation days in three years," Aaron told Captain Dave Billingsley later that afternoon at the Sheriff's Department. He glanced through the glass window separating the captain's office from the deputies' bullpen, reassuring himself that Melissa was still sitting in the chair beside his empty desk.

"You want time off so you can keep an eye on Melissa Draper," Billingsley said, cutting through the crap as neatly as he usually did.

"I think someone's trying to kill her."

"You're a deputy, not a bodyguard," Billingsley pointed out, although Aaron could tell by the tone of his voice that the burly rusty-haired captain wasn't trying to dissuade him so much as he was warning Aaron to be careful about how he approached the task of protecting Melissa Draper.

Don't get personally involved with a victim.

It was a major "don't" of law enforcement. Careers could be ruined by affairs with needy victims.

But need wasn't what drew him to Melissa, he assured himself. He was just intrigued by the mystery she posed.

"You can have a week," Billingsley said. "It goes against your vacation time. But as far as I'm concerned, you're still investigating the arson case as well as the shooting. So if you find anything, report it just like you're on the job. Got it?"

"Yes, sir."

Outside, Melissa stood as he came out of the captain's office. "He told you it's a stupid idea, right?"

"You don't have to be quite so eager to be shed of me," he said, grabbing the coat she'd draped over the back of her chair. He helped her into it. "And actually, he gave me the time off."

"I just think this is a bad idea." Her brow creased with worry. "I'm used to living alone—"

"I won't be any more trouble than Jasper. Probably less." He gestured toward the exit. "Come on, let's go. We can sort out the details—"

"Melissa?" A woman's voice rose over the bullpen chatter. Aaron saw Melissa's eyes widen as her head whipped up.

A pretty woman in her late fifties with sandy brown hair approached hurriedly, her gaze fixed on Melissa's face. She caught Melissa up in a fierce hug as soon as she reached her. "Thank God you're okay."

"Mom?"

Mrs. Draper pulled back, holding Melissa at arm's length as if checking her over for injuries. She winced at the bruises on Melissa's neck. "I saw the article in the paper. About that terrible man. Why didn't you call me?"

"I'm not really hurt." Melissa looked up at Aaron. He got the odd feeling that she was asking him for rescue. But from what? Her own mother?

Mrs. Draper followed Melissa's gaze. "Sorry—did I interrupt something?"

Melissa cleared her throat, her spine going ramrod straight. "Mom, this is Aaron Cooper. Aaron, this is my mother, Karen Draper."

Aaron shook the older woman's hand. "Pleased to meet you."

"Aaron and I were just about to head out—"

"Ah. This is the young man, isn't he?"

To Aaron's surprise, Melissa slipped her hand into his, twining her small fingers with his.

"Yes," she said to her mother. "Aaron's my boyfriend."

Chapter Eight

Melissa's heart sank the second the word *boyfriend* escaped her lips. She tried to pull her hand from Aaron's, but he tightened his fingers, trapping her hand in place.

Her mother was smiling at Aaron with delight, no doubt surprised that her mousy daughter had managed to snag someone like Aaron Cooper. "I'm so happy to meet you finally, Aaron. Melissa's father and I have been wondering when she was going to bring you to Christmas at our house this time around."

Aaron gave Melissa a quick, quizzical look, but when he turned back to smile at Melissa's mother, he seemed completely in control. "I hated to miss meeting you this past Christmas, but my brother Luke was back home after ten years away—he was in the Marines—and, well, my mother would have thrown an unholy fit if I didn't come to Christmas at her house."

"Unholy fit, huh?" Melissa's mother smiled. "Apparently that's what I'm doing wrong." She gave Melissa a gentle but pointed look. "Nothing I do seems to get Melissa home for a visit these days."

Aaron lifted Melissa's hand to his lips, the light touch sending an electric shock racing down her spine. She looked up at him, trying to clear the sudden fog out of her brain.

"I'm afraid that's my fault, too, at least where Christmas

is concerned," Aaron said. "She mentioned trying to drop by your house later in the day, but Luke was late arriving, and I confess, I wanted him to meet her. You know, show her off a little. Do you forgive me?"

Melissa almost rolled her eyes at the overkill, but her mother seemed utterly charmed.

"All is forgiven, under one condition," Karen said. "Have dinner with us tomorrow night. I know Melissa's father will be happy to meet you."

Melissa felt a cold chill wash over her, driving away the lingering warmth of Aaron's body next to hers.

No, she thought. *No, no, no—*

"Of course," Aaron answered.

Melissa thought she was going to throw up.

"Six o'clock okay?"

"Sounds great."

Karen turned her attention back to Melissa. "Your dad said to tell you he thinks you're very brave."

The nausea in her stomach roiled wildly. She managed a weak smile and a nod. "Aaron and I have to go, Mom."

"I'll walk you out," Karen said, as Melissa had known she would. Because, apparently, surviving a murder attempt wasn't enough stress for one day.

To her relief, Aaron kept her mother distracted with small talk, pouring on the charm. By the time they reached her mother's car in the guest parking area, Karen was a full-fledged member of Team Aaron.

"So," Aaron said a few minutes later as he opened the passenger door of his truck for her, "are you going to tell me why that very nice woman freaked the hell out of you just now?"

Melissa climbed into the cab without answering, making a show of belting herself in while Aaron waited in the open door.

"She doesn't freak me out," she said finally, when it was clear he wasn't going to move until she answered.

Aaron just looked at her, disbelief infusing every inch of his expression. When she said nothing more, he closed the door and rounded the truck to climb behind the wheel.

"You were turning green by the time we got out of there," he said quietly, buckling his own seat belt.

"Your cop instincts are way off this time," she lied. Not that she thought he'd believe her, but it was worth a try.

Aaron paused with his hand on the ignition, turning to look at her. "You're the one who pulled the boyfriend card, not me. So deal with it. If I'm going over to your parents' house tomorrow night to play the loving boyfriend, I think I have a right to know what I'm up against."

"I shouldn't have done that. I don't know why I did."

"I can guess." Aaron sat back, leaving the keys in the ignition without starting the truck. "At some point, not long ago, you told your mother you had a boyfriend to get out of some family obligation, right? Used him as an excuse for why you couldn't show up for Thanksgiving or Christmas—"

"Or both," she muttered.

"Why the subterfuge?"

"It's complicated."

"Then maybe I should know a little bit about it, since I'm going to be playing Romeo to your Juliet tomorrow night."

Melissa pressed her fingertips against her throbbing temples. "I can't stand visiting my parents. It's physically uncomfortable for me. So I made up an excuse for why I couldn't make it home for the holidays."

Aaron frowned at her, clearly trying to understand. "Your mother is a very nice woman. Your father's a great guy—"

"No, he's not," she snapped.

Silence swallowed the echo of her angry words. She looked down at her hands, tears burning like acid behind her eyes.

"What are you saying, Melissa?" Aaron reached across the seat and caught her chin with gentle fingers. He coaxed her to look at him, his gaze concerned.

"He hits her," she blurted, her voice soft and small, like the child she'd been the first time she'd seen her father backhand her mother during one of their frequent arguments.

Aaron let go of her chin, his expression stunned and disbelieving. "What?"

A hot ache settled in her chest. "I know what you're thinking. He's a pillar of the community. Former sheriff's deputy, coached little league, never missed a day of church—"

"Did he hit you, too?"

She looked up, surprised by the tension in his voice. His eyes flashed silver fire, anger lining his strong, masculine features. For a second, she was reminded of his violent reaction when Terry Harris had gone after her, but this time she also saw the iron control he had over his anger. It simmered but showed no signs of boiling over.

"No, he never hit me," she answered.

"Why didn't anyone know what he was doing to your mother?"

She grimaced. "He was a deputy. He knew where to hit her to hide the bruises."

"The broken arm you were talking about earlier—"

"He knocked her down the front steps."

"My God."

"I told people a couple of times. They thought I was just being a typical rebellious kid. My mother never admitted any of it, and everybody thought so highly of my dad—"

"God, I told you I became a cop because of your father." Aaron ran his hand over his jaw, his palm rasping softly against his beard stubble. "Bet you loved hearing that."

"It happens that way sometimes," she said. "They compartmentalize their lives. To everybody else, they really are great guys. Because they have a punching bag at home to take out their frustrations on."

"He still hits her?"

"I can't imagine he's stopped. He's not the kind of man who'd seek help. And those who don't usually keep hitting."

Aaron released a long breath. "I'm sorry. I wish—I wish you'd told me years ago."

"It wasn't the kind of thing I talked about." Not after the first few attempts to tell the truth. It had been easier to keep her head down and do what she could to protect her mother from as much of the abuse as she could.

"And I wasn't the kind of guy you could have told, even if you did talk about it," he said grimly. "I'm sorry for that."

She believed him. "I don't want to have dinner at my parents' house tomorrow."

"I don't blame you. But I think maybe we should."

She looked at him, anxiety bubbling in her gut. "Why?"

"Because it might help for your father to know that there's someone watching him now."

She shook her head, horrified by the thought. "You can't confront him."

"I'm not sure I'd need to."

"But you would. You'd fly off the handle at the first provocation—"

The look he shot her was pained. "Is that how you see me?"

She stared back at him, not sure how to answer. Was that how she really saw him, as some sort of hothead who couldn't be trusted to keep his fists to himself at the first sign of confrontation? She'd thought so yesterday, when he'd been pinning Terry Harris to the ground with a forearm to the throat, but the Aaron Cooper who'd sat here and listened to her confess one of her darkest secrets had been gentle. Sweet, even. Quick to understand and ready to take her side.

She'd felt comfortable enough to seek his protection after she escaped Terry's attack. Certain enough today to call him when the shots rang out.

"No," she said aloud. "That's not how I see you."

He didn't look convinced but went back to his original argument. "I think your father should know there's another man in the family who's not going to put up with anybody knocking your mother around."

"But you're not really in the family."

"He won't know that."

She managed a smile. "You're sweet to offer to keep up the charade, but I shouldn't have put you in that position in the first place. It's my mess. I'll deal with it."

"You have enough to worry about right now. Don't add any more stress to your life." He reached across the truck cab and patted the back of her hand where it lay on the seat. "Let's just go to dinner tomorrow night. We don't have to stay long."

She felt a niggle of unease. "Why do you want to go? To see for yourself that I'm telling you the truth?"

"I believe you're telling the truth. But I told your mother I'd be there for dinner, and I don't like the idea of her telling your father there's company coming for nothing."

He had a point. Her father had usually discouraged her mother and her from having people over to visit at the house. The self-imposed isolation had probably been a contributing factor to her own social awkwardness, come to think of it.

It had taken a lot of courage for her mother to extend Aaron the invitation without consulting her father. She didn't want her mother to have to deal with the fallout alone if they stood her up.

She sighed. "Okay. We'll go to dinner tomorrow night."

But she couldn't shake the feeling that she'd regret it.

"WANT ANOTHER PIECE?" Aaron waved a slice of pizza in front of Melissa's face.

She groaned. "No, please, I'm stuffed."

He tossed the slice back into the box. "Didn't eat much."

She laughed. "Two pieces may not be much in Aaron World, but in Melissa World—"

He reached for her plate just as she did, their hands brushing. Heat flowed into her fingers where they touched.

"I'll do the dishes." He took the plate.

"Okay, I'll put up the leftovers."

"Cold pizza, the breakfast of champions." With a grin, Aaron started water running in the sink. While waiting for the sink to fill, he reached over and turned on a small radio sitting on the counter by the toaster. A slow country ballad filled the small kitchen.

"Man, that brings back memories." Aaron looked over at Melissa. "Senior Prom, remember?"

She shook her head. "Never went to the prom."

"Oh. You didn't?" He looked surprised.

"Nope. Nobody ever asked, and who wants to go alone?"

"Nobody ever asked you? Really? What kind of idiots went to that school?" His look of disbelief was sort of flattering.

Idiots like you, she thought, hiding a smile.

"Well, anyway, this was the song they played when the king and queen of the prom danced their first dance after the coronation."

"I didn't think guys remembered things like that." She put the bag of leftovers in the refrigerator.

"We don't, usually. But Kelly Rayburn dumped me right

in the middle of the dance. Knocked that stupid crown off my head and stomped it to shreds right there on the gym floor." He laughed. "I deserved it—she'd caught me flirting with Angie Logan at the punch bowl, although in my defense, who wouldn't flirt with Angie Logan?"

"You're terrible."

"I was a teenage boy."

"As I was saying."

He nudged her with his elbow. "You should have come to the prom alone. I could have used a dance partner after that."

As if he'd ever have asked her to dance. "What, Angie didn't jump right in once you were free?"

"No, of course not. That would have made her look easy."

"So she waited until after the prom?"

He grinned again. "Yeah."

"So terrible."

"So what did you do prom night instead of watching my abject humiliation?" He turned off the tap and transferred the dirty plates from the counter to the water. "Homework?"

"No. I always did that during my study periods." She leaned against the counter. "I tried to spend as much time with my mom as I could."

His voice lost its teasing tone. "As a buffer?"

She looked up to find him watching her, sympathy in his gray eyes. "Yes."

"I guess things like the prom probably didn't mean that much to you in comparison."

Blinking back unexpected tears, she picked up a dish towel and dried the plate he'd just rinsed, buying time to regain control before she responded.

"I wanted to go to the prom," she said quietly, reaching for the next plate. "I wanted to go to the homecoming dance.

I wanted to be in the stands for football games and try out for cheerleading, even though I'd have been terrible. I would have loved to have done all those things, but—"

"But you didn't dare spend that much time away from home."

"Some kids do anything they can to get away. That's how they deal with it. I dealt with it by becoming my mother's protector, the best I could."

"How did they ever get you to leave home for college?"

"My mother told me I was making the situation worse. I don't know, maybe I was." She shook her head, remembering the pain of her mother's harsh statements. "But I think she just wanted me out of that house. She didn't want me trapped there for the rest of my life."

Aaron drained the sink and reached for the dishtowel bunched between her hands. He wiped his hands dry and laid the towel on the counter. "So you finally left?"

"I thought when I went to college, when I was finally on my own, I'd become a different person. And I did, for a while." She pressed her lips to a hard line, remembering the consequences of her sudden freedom. "But you can't really change who you are, can you?"

"I think you can," he said with conviction.

"Yeah? How, exactly, do you do that?"

He shrugged. "I think that's a matter for you to figure out for yourself. But I know people can make big changes in the way they choose to live their lives. I've seen it."

"When have you seen it?" she challenged.

"When my brother Sam met Kristen Tandy."

Melissa flinched. The name Tandy was as notorious in Chickasaw County as any. Sixteen years ago, a woman named Molly Jane Tandy had murdered four of her five children. Her daughter Kristen had been the only survivor. "How'd she change?"

"Kristen had a lot of issues to work through to be with Sam and Maddy. But she did it. She overcame her fear and let herself love my niece Maddy and trust Sam enough to marry him."

"I heard about the kidnapping attempt, but I didn't realize she and your brother were married—"

"It was a small wedding. I don't think they even announced it in the paper." Aaron crossed to where she stood, lifting her chin with the tip of his finger. "If someone who went through what Kristen went through can change herself—"

"You think anyone can," Melissa finished for him, a lump in her throat. As much as she'd been through in her life, it paled compared to what Kristen had gone through. "I don't think people really change very much from who they are. Wife batterers rarely stop hitting the women in their lives. Sex offenders don't stop raping and molesting."

"Wallflowers don't learn to let down their hair and boogie?" he countered with a smile.

She frowned at him. "You're making fun of me."

His smile faded. "I'm just saying there's a difference between overcoming pathology and overcoming shyness."

She wasn't sure why she was arguing with him. In a lot of important ways, she *had* changed her own life, hadn't she? She'd stopped letting things happen to her, for one thing, taking charge of her life, living on her own terms.

It was only when it came to relationships with men that she'd locked the door and thrown away the key. And that fear was about a whole lot more than simple shyness.

The song on the radio changed again, to another ballad. Aaron gave her an odd look.

"What?" she asked. "Another prom song?"

He shook his head. "Actually, I just remembered something about you from high school."

She gave him a wary look. "Sure you're not thinking of Dina Pritchard again?"

"Positive." He stepped closer, closing the distance between them. "Do you remember freshman year, the first mixer?"

"Actually, yes," she said. "The only dance I ever got to go to. Dad was out of town at some law enforcement seminar." She smiled at the memory. "Mom and I treated the whole three days like a slumber party. Stayed up late, did each other's nails, ate junk. It was great."

"I remember you from the dance."

She shook her head. "Nobody asked me to dance. I stood by the wall all night, watching everybody else."

Aaron smiled. "I saw you standing by the wall. You were wearing something really simple. I don't remember the color or anything, but it made you stand out from everyone else in their ruffles and satin."

"It was blue," she said. "Something of my mother's, from when she was in high school."

He nodded. "I didn't do any dancing that night, either. My mom forced me to go to keep an eye on Gabe and Jake and their dates."

Melissa smiled. "How'd that go?"

"Like herding cats."

She chuckled.

"I didn't dare ask anyone to dance. My brothers would've ragged on me for days. So I hung with the rest of the junior varsity squad cutting up and making fun of everyone else."

"Ah, the noisy group over in the corner by the punch bowl."

"Guilty as charged."

"At least you were having fun."

"You weren't, I suppose."

"I don't know." She gave a little shrug. "It was fun to get out of the house. I liked the music."

"That's what I remember about you." He leaned a little closer to her, lowering his voice. "You may have been standing by the wall, but your body loved the music. I couldn't look away. It was like you were dancing from the inside out."

His low voice was sheer seduction, reeling her in until she swayed toward him, the distance between them closing despite the warning bells clanging loudly in her head.

Aaron took her hand. "Dance with me."

She fell into step with him as he wrapped one arm around her waist, drawing her close. "I'm not much of a dancer," she murmured, her whole body going hot and tingly.

"I saw you," he said in a half whisper that sent electricity darting up her spine. "I know better."

On the radio, the song switched to something more upbeat, but Aaron didn't change the slow tempo of their dance, which had settled into little more than a rhythmic embrace. Melissa gave up her inner struggle and relaxed, enjoying the feel of Aaron's body, warm and strong, against hers.

What if he'd asked her to dance that night at the fall mixer? Would it have changed anything that had happened afterwards?

Probably not. But it would have been a good memory to pull out from the back of her mind now and then.

Just like this dance. Nothing more might come of dancing here in the guest cottage kitchen with Aaron Cooper. Maybe nothing more should. But she could look back on this moment and remember that once, Aaron Cooper wanted to dance with her. Twice, if he was telling the truth about that long ago night.

She could use all the good memories she could get.

A trilling noise cut through the hum of contentment buzzing through Melissa's brain. Aaron groaned, the sound rumbling through her chest where their bodies met. "My phone," he said.

He stepped away from her. Cool air filled the void between them, making her shiver.

He crossed to the radio, shutting it off as he took the call. He listened a couple of seconds, speaking too low for her to hear. Finally, he hung up, turning back to look at Melissa. All softness was gone from his features.

Her stomach fluttered. "What is it?"

His lips flattened to a tight line. "Why didn't you tell me your college boyfriend damned near killed you?"

Chapter Nine

The look of horrified shame on Melissa's face made Aaron's chest hurt. "Technically, he was my law school boyfriend."

"Whatever."

"I didn't want to discuss it," she said defensively, her eyes bright with unshed tears.

He swallowed his anger, realizing she thought his fury was directed at her instead of the son of a bitch who'd landed her in a North Carolina hospital for almost six weeks. "I'm sorry. I'm not upset with you. I just think it's pertinent information, given the two recent attempts on your life."

She shook her head. "Evan's in prison."

"Actually, he's not."

Her head snapped up. "What? The judge gave him seven to ten, and he's done only four years."

"Apparently the North Carolina penal system has a funding shortfall and paroled several first offenders with good behavior who'd done at least half their minimum sentence. He got out a week ago." Aaron pocketed his cell phone.

After a moment of tense silence, she asked, "How did you find out about Evan?"

"We started a background check the morning of the fire. We just got something back from our query to North Carolina. That was Riley on the phone."

She gave a bleak huff of laughter. "I forgot I was once your prime suspect."

"Riley's trying to get contact information for his parole officer, but we probably can't even get the process started before tomorrow." Aaron eased across the room to where she stood, careful not to spook her. She looked wound tight, ready to fight or flee. "I know you probably don't want to even think about the bastard, but is it possible he held enough of a grudge to break parole to come after you again?"

She shot him a pained look. "I don't know. Sometimes I think I didn't know him at all."

"Had you been together long?"

"Eight months. We were already talking about getting engaged." She smoothed her hair back, her hands shaking. "I know it's a total cliché, but he really was a sweet guy at first. Remembered my birthday, all the silly little anniversaries. He'd bring me flowers for no reason and made me feel beautiful."

The pain in her eyes made Aaron want to hit something. But rage was the last thing she needed from him. "Let's sit, okay?"

She followed him into the living room and sat on the sofa, hunching a little as if she felt the need to protect herself. He bypassed the cushion beside her and settled in the armchair just to her right, waiting for her to gather her thoughts though he was impatient to know everything she'd gone through, as if by hearing it he could somehow fix the damage done.

As if it were fixable.

But maybe telling him everything would, in a small way, relieve her of some of the burden she obviously still carried.

"It changed once we became…intimate." She darted him a quick look.

He met her gaze and offered silent encouragement, ignoring a strange churning sensation in his gut.

Her pale cheeks growing pink, she continued. "It wasn't exactly like flipping a switch—he was really subtle about it for a while. Popping in to see me without warning, calling me all the time. We were dating seriously, so I didn't really recognize it for what it was until it was almost too late."

"He was stalking you."

She nodded. "Weird to think a guy you're thinking about marrying could be your stalker. But that's how it began to feel." Her hands twined together in her lap, twisting and flexing. "I asked him to give me more room to breathe and he got angry. He accused me of trying to back out of the relationship. I don't know—maybe I was, a little. I stopped talking about marriage at that point."

"Did he start accusing you of cheating?"

"Oh, yeah. The sad thing was, at first, I was flattered by his jealousy. I wasn't used to being wanted that way." Her soft laugh held no hint of humor. "Pathetic, huh?"

"No. Everybody wants to be wanted." He laid his hand over hers. She gave a little twitch at his touch but her restless hand stilled. "You're no more pathetic than the rest of us."

He could see she didn't quite believe him. He couldn't blame her. He knew he had a reputation around Chickasaw County as a player, the guy who couldn't be tamed. He'd earned it, fair and square, hadn't he? But guys who couldn't be tamed usually ended up alone.

He was no exception, he was afraid. It wasn't something he was proud of. But damned if he could figure out how to change.

"When did he turn violent?" he asked.

"It started with fits of anger. Punching the wall, kicking over the coffee table. He didn't hit me, so I told myself that it was a good thing, that he could control his anger enough not to physically hurt me."

"Then he started destroying things you cared about," Aaron guessed. He'd investigated abuse cases before. He'd seen the patterns of escalation.

"Tore up books. Broke CDs. Smashed my television. Thank God I didn't have any pets at the time."

"Did you try to break up with him?"

"Of course." She smiled bitterly. "Then he turned back into the sweet guy I'd fallen in love with in the first place. Promised he'd get control of himself and make it up to me. I wanted to believe him, so I did. I thought I was lucky. At least Evan didn't hit me. As long as he wasn't hitting me, he was still way ahead of my father. "

"Until he did hit you."

"That ended the relationship," she said, her voice threaded with steel. "I may have overlooked the signs of escalation, but I wasn't going to overlook being backhanded by the man who swore he loved me."

"So you broke it off and he retaliated?"

"He broke into my apartment one night, a couple of weeks after I ended it and attacked me while I was still asleep. He pulled me out of bed and threw me around. When I fought back, he dragged me out to the apartment balcony and tried to throw me off." She looked down at her lap, where Aaron's hand still lay over hers. "I caught onto the railing."

Riley had given Aaron a condensed version of the injuries Melissa had sustained—severe head trauma, several broken ribs, a collapsed lung, a broken femur, broken fingers. The report hadn't detailed how she'd sustained the injuries. "How long did you hold on?" he asked, horrified.

Melissa shuddered. "Until Evan started beating my fingers with a brass candlestick."

Just picturing the scenario in his mind made Aaron want

Send For
2 FREE BOOKS
Today!

I accept your offer!

Please send me two
free Harlequin Intrigue®
novels and two mystery
gifts (gifts worth about $10).
I understand that these books
are completely free—even
the shipping and handling will
be paid—and I am under no
obligation to purchase anything, ever,
as explained on the back of this card.

About how many NEW paperback fiction books have you purchased in the past 3 months?

❑ 0-2	❑ 3-6	❑ 7 or more
E7ZM	**E7LN**	**E7LY**

❑ I prefer the regular-print edition
182/382 HDL

❑ I prefer the larger-print edition
199/399 HDL

Please Print

FIRST NAME

LAST NAME

ADDRESS

APT.#   CITY

STATE/PROV.   ZIP/POSTAL CODE

Visit us online at
www.ReaderService.com

H-I-09/10

NO POSTAGE
NECESSARY
IF MAILED
IN THE
UNITED STATES

BUSINESS REPLY MAIL
FIRST-CLASS MAIL   PERMIT NO. 717   BUFFALO, NY

POSTAGE WILL BE PAID BY ADDRESSEE

THE READER SERVICE
PO BOX 1867
BUFFALO NY 14240-9952

to hunt Hallman down and make him pay in blood. He forced back his fury so that his voice was calm when he spoke. "Here's the big question, I guess. Do you think he could have set your house on fire or shot at your car? Does that seem like something he'd do? Was that his M.O.?"

He saw her mind working behind her troubled blue eyes. After a moment, her shoulders hunched upwards in defeat. "I don't know. He was always spontaneous in his rages. Not calculated. Even the final attack—he didn't plan what he was going to do enough to bring a gun or a knife. He used what he found in my apartment. I don't think he even wanted me dead at first—at least, that wasn't the real reason for the attack. It was more visceral for him. He wanted his hands on me, to mete out the punishment he believed I deserved. A gun or a knife would end things too quickly. Too—impersonally."

"Well, I'll tell you what." He gave her hand a squeeze. "Riley and I are going to get together and track him down. We'll find out where he is and what he's doing. Okay?"

She released a shaky breath. "Okay."

"Thank you for telling me about this," Aaron said. He started to let go of her hand, but she turned it palm upwards, her fingers closing around his. He met her gaze, finding her eyes warm and liquid.

"It's been hard for me to talk about this with anyone." Moisture glittered in her eyes, hard and cold like diamonds, but didn't fall. She pulled her hand from his. "You made it easier than I expected."

"I hate that all this happened to you." Thinking about someone abusing her trust and her loyalty made him ill. He wished he'd been there to protect her.

She gave him a faint smile. "It's been a long couple of days. I could use some sleep."

He rose with her, his gaze fixed on her slumped shoulders as she trudged down the short hallway to her bedroom.

He suspected she wasn't so much sleepy as emotionally exhausted, in need of retreat. He was feeling pretty wiped out himself.

But he still had work to do tonight.

He was going to make damned sure that bastard never got his hands on Melissa again, whatever it took.

"I'VE CHANGED MY MIND." Melissa stopped halfway up the flagstone path and turned back toward the car.

Aaron's warm fingers closed over hers. "Are you sure? I still think this is a good idea, but you want to chicken out—"

She slanted a glare at him. "Don't try to shame me into going through with this."

He gave her hand a light squeeze and let it go. "I'm not, really. If you don't want to do it, I'll take you right back to the cottage. I just want you to be sure."

She opened her mouth to assure him she knew what she wanted, but nothing came out. She pressed her lips closed, her mind holding an internal debate about whether or not having dinner with her parents was a good idea. Before she came to a conclusion, the front door opened and her mother stepped out onto the porch, beaming at her and Aaron with so much happiness Melissa knew she couldn't back out now.

She caught Aaron's hand and headed up the porch steps. "We brought dessert."

Aaron let go of Melissa's hand and gave Karen Draper the deep-dish peach cobbler Melissa had spent the afternoon making. She knew it was her mother's favorite, and Beth Cooper had been generous enough to share some of the peach preserves she'd canned earlier that year from the bounty of the three peach trees that grew on the lakeside property. It had been awhile since Melissa had baked anything, but Aaron had sampled a small bite and assured her it was delicious.

She'd been too nervous to sample it herself to find out if he was just being kind.

"You didn't have to, but thank you." Karen gestured toward the door. "Come in. Your father is setting the table."

Melissa blinked. Setting the table? Since when had her father ever set the table?

Aaron's hand pressed firmly against the small of her back, nudging her forward when her feet faltered. "Is there anything we can do to help?" he asked politely.

"Just enjoy yourselves," Karen said with a smile. She led them through the neat, simply-furnished living room into the dining room, where Melissa's father, Derek, was setting a large pitcher of iced tea in the center of the round oak table.

He looked up at their entrance, his gaze locking with Melissa's. The intensity in his blue eyes, so like her own, set off a wild flutter of apprehension in the center of her belly.

His gaze left her, finally, to meet Aaron's. Derek's smile seemed genuine. "Aaron Cooper. I hear you finally gave up your life of crime."

Aaron's smile in response was guarded. "Yes, sir, I did." Melissa sensed that he had said much less than he might have wanted—trying to be on his best behavior, as she'd asked.

"And as for you, Missy Mae—"

She flinched at her father's use of his favorite nickname for her.

"I swear you've been getting into more trouble now than when you were a teenager." His tone was stern, but his eyes were gentle. He almost looked proud of her. She blinked again, wondering if she was imagining things.

"She seems to be a trouble magnet." Aaron laid his hand gently against her spine, as if he recognized her need for his moral support. His voice hardened a notch. "That's why I'm keeping a close eye on her these days. I don't intend to let anyone hurt her—or anyone she cares about."

Melissa glanced at her mother. Karen was looking at her with an expression somewhere between hope and fear. "Melissa, I could actually use your help in the kitchen for a moment. Derek, weren't you dying to ask Aaron something about your new boat?" She gave Melissa's father a pointed look.

No, Melissa thought. No way was she going to let Aaron be alone with her father for even a second. "But aren't we about to have dinner?" she protested.

"The pot roast isn't quite done," her mother answered placidly, glancing toward Melissa's father as if waiting for him to back her up.

They were conspiring with each other? Against her? What in the hell was going on? Melissa looked desperately at Aaron.

He met her gaze, puzzlement in his gray eyes, but when her father clapped him on the shoulder and gestured toward the back door Aaron went with him.

Melissa wheeled on her mother. "Are you crazy?"

Her mother smiled. "No. I'm just tired of waiting for you to start listening to what I've been trying to tell you."

Melissa bristled. "I don't want to hear how he's changed. Abusers don't just get better."

Karen's smile faded. "No, they don't. Not without help."

"Like Dad's going to get any help."

"He did get help."

Melissa stared at her mother. Was she so desperate to pretend things were okay that she'd lie about something so impossible? Seeking help was the last thing Derek Draper would do. His pride wouldn't allow it. "Stop lying to me, Mom. Stop lying to yourself."

"You can speak to his counselor if you like. Probably not

tonight, since it's after office hours, but Derek could call the treatment center tomorrow and give his counselor permission to discuss his case with you," Karen said quietly.

Melissa groped for a nearby chair and sat, her knees trembling. Either her mother had completely lost her sanity, or her father had actually sought help for his abusive behavior.

Right now she was betting on insanity.

"I understand why you're confused," Karen said.

"When was this treatment supposed to have happened?"

"Shortly after your father's retirement."

"Four years ago?"

Karen pulled up another chair and sat across from her, reaching out to touch Melissa's hand. "He did it as much for you as for me, you know."

"For me? I was gone."

"At the time he made the decision, you were in the hospital fighting for your life." Karen squeezed Melissa's hand, her fingers warm and firm. "When he saw what Evan did to you, it was like—" She paused, as if struggling for the right words. "It was like he saw himself in the mirror. What he'd become. What he was doing."

Tears burned at the back of Melissa's eyes, but she fought them, blinking hard. "That's crazy. Why couldn't he look at *you* and see what he was doing? You were the one with the bruises long before I was hurt."

Her mother let go of her hand, pressing her fingertips to her own lips. Tears sparkled in her eyes. "He couldn't let himself see me. If he did, he'd have had to stop hitting me. And in some ways, hitting me was the only thing that let him be normal in all the other parts of his life."

Melissa's stomach twisted, nausea hot in her throat. "That's sick, Mom. Can't you hear how sick that is?"

"I know it's sick," Karen agreed. "I had my own reasons

for letting him hurt me. In some ways, I had as much to work through as he did, once we got help."

Melissa shook her head, not believing any of what she was hearing. It was crazy. Impossible. "What did he do? Go to some mental health doc-in-the-box and say, 'Hey, I hit my wife and she kind of digs it. Can you fix us?'"

"That's uncalled for," Karen said.

"Is it?" Melissa pushed to her feet, then sat back down as her trembling knees threatened to buckle. "How am I supposed to believe any of this, after what I watched happen day after day for eighteen years?"

"Aaron Cooper isn't your boyfriend, is he?"

Melissa blinked, thrown by the change in subject. "What?"

"More to the point," her mother continued, "You don't have a boyfriend. You haven't had one since Evan."

"What does that have to do with you and Dad?"

The look her mother gave her was so pained, Melissa almost winced. "I think it has everything to do with it. I think it has everything to do with why you let Evan Hallman stick around about six months longer than you should have."

Melissa laughed grimly, her stomach reduced to one hot, painful knot. "You mean that your dysfunctional relationship ruined me for a healthy one of my own?" An image of Aaron Cooper flashed through her mind, distorted by the afterimage of Evan Hallman's rage-maddened visage burned permanently in her brain. "What else did you expect?"

"I don't think it's ruined you. Not yet." Karen reached out and caught Melissa's hand.

Melissa pulled her hand back, twining her fingers together in her lap. "And what's supposed to save me? You and me and Daddy holding hands together and singing happy songs over and over until we're finally one nondysfunctional family?"

"No."

"Then what? What's going to save me from a life of bitter spinsterhood, Mom?"

"Forgiving your father."

"LET'S JUST cut to the chase, son. I know you know what I used to do to Melissa's mother, so let's just get it out there in the open." Derek Draper didn't even wait for them to reach the shiny new Triton bass boat hooked to the red Ford pick-up truck before he dropped the pretext for leaving the house.

Aaron folded his arms across his chest, remaining silent as he looked down at Draper. If the abusive bastard thought he was going to make things any easier on him, he was a fool.

Draper's lips curved slightly. "About what I thought." He resumed walking toward the boat, leaving Aaron to follow.

Aaron kept pace at a slight distance, remembering his promise to Melissa to control his temper, even though he wanted nothing more than to show Derek Draper what it was like to be on the losing end of a beating.

But he wasn't about to stoop to Draper's level. No matter what Melissa might believe about his temper, Aaron wasn't the kind of man who solved his problems with his fists.

"Not going to speak?" Draper turned to look at him. He didn't look defiant, exactly. Nor did he seem conciliatory. He just looked…sad.

"What's there to say? That you're a cowardly son of a bitch who hits his wife? I reckon you know that about yourself already." Aaron grimaced. "But I'll tell you this—if I ever get a whiff of proof about what you're doing, I'll haul your sorry butt to jail faster than you can spit."

Draper's lips curved into an unexpected smile. "Believe it or not, Aaron, that's exactly what I hoped you'd say."

Chapter Ten

"Your father loves you, Melissa. He always did. It was one of the reasons you were able to be a buffer between us." Karen Draper's expression reflected her pain. "I let you do that far too long. I kept you close, didn't encourage you to go out and learn how to live your own life until it was almost too late. Then, I pushed you out of the nest so cruelly—"

So she'd been right. Her mother had lied to her to get her to leave. "You should have come with me."

Karen shook her head sadly. "I know you don't understand. It seems like another person—another life—when I think back on it. But I loved your father. I didn't want to leave him." She sat in the chair Melissa had refused, lifting one hand to her cheek. "I thought the abuse was a fair price to pay for it."

Melissa reached for another chair and pulled it up next to her mother's. "You know how twisted that is."

Karen nodded. "Your father wasn't the only one who saw a counselor." She reached for Melissa's hand. "I never told you your grandfather was abusive. To all of us."

Melissa stared at her mother, her stomach knotting.

"You were so little when he died, I thought it would be better if you never knew. So I didn't tell you."

Protecting another abuser. Her mother's actions were beginning to make a horrible sort of sense.

"My father punished me because he loved me. So did your father. That's how I saw it." Karen gave a terrible laugh.

Melissa shook her head. "I had no idea."

"But when you were born—I knew it wasn't right." Karen looked at her hands. "I could take the slaps and punches, but I was so afraid he'd hit you instead. So I antagonized him more after you were born."

Melissa looked at her mother, horrified. "To keep him focused on you instead of me."

"But I know now your father would never have hit you. He was different in that way from your grandfather." Karen looked up at her. "You defied him so much when you were a teenager, trying to protect me, but he never laid a hand on you. Did he?"

Melissa shook her head. She'd wondered about that, sometimes, why he'd hit her mother so readily but never raised a hand to her. Not that it made any difference. Hitting her mother was horrible enough.

"I can't be the one to tell you what made your father do what he did. It's something he'll have to tell you on his own, when you're both ready," Karen added.

Melissa stood again, her whole body trembling with the violent urge to run as far away from this house as she could get. Her mother had given her a lot to think about. Too much.

It was all too much.

Grabbing her purse from the table, she pushed past her mother and headed for the front door.

"So you got help and now it's okay?" Aaron frowned at Draper, annoyed at being ambushed and even more annoyed at himself for beginning to fall for what the man was telling him. In his job, he saw how few men really stopped hitting the women they abused. Though treatment helped some of them, many abused again within a few months of treatment.

But Draper sounded as if he was telling the truth.

"I can't describe what it was like," Draper said, rubbing his lean jaw. "Standing there over my baby girl's hospital bed, looking down at this—this thing I couldn't even recognize because her face was so bruised and swollen from what that bastard did to her. It was—" Draper paused, licking his lips.

Aaron saw him struggling with emotion. He tried to keep his own emotional distance, maintain professional skepticism, but what Draper was telling him was so vivid, so close to his own worst imaginings of what Melissa had gone through, that he found it hard to remain unaffected.

He could picture her, battered and barely clinging to life. He'd seen people in that state before, known the harrowing sensation of counting heartbeats with the fervent hope that they'd keep coming for a few more minutes, a few more hours, a few more days.

"It was like looking at myself in a mirror," Draper said quietly. "The ugliness of what Hallman did to her—I saw myself in that violence. I saw my own brutality, my rage and pain. I saw what I'd become. What my family had made me."

Aaron darted a look at Draper.

The man met his gaze, but only with effort. He looked haunted. "Things happened to me when I was just a kid. Terrible things."

Aaron felt ill. Draper didn't have to go into detail for Aaron to know it had been bad. He could see the man's agony in his eyes.

"I know it doesn't excuse anything. I had a choice. A lot of people go through what I did, or worse, and don't end up hurting the people they love."

"No, they don't."

"I went the day after that hospital visit and asked for help. And I got it."

"Did you go into a treatment facility?" Aaron asked.

"For about a month." He grimaced. "And I still got out of there before Melissa got out of the hospital."

Aaron pressed his lips to a thin line, wondering what he should say. Congratulations for not beating your wife any longer? He settled on an important question. "Any lapses since you left treatment?"

"I haven't left treatment. I still go to outpatient counseling," Draper answered. "But to answer your question, no. No lapses. I struggled with it early on, in the first few months. I was facing hard memories and there was a lot of stress. But I never hit her again." He looked up, meeting Aaron's gaze squarely, a ghost of a smile gracing his mouth. "These days, I don't ever want to. I love that woman. I always did, you know."

Aaron had no problem being skeptical about Draper's declaration. He'd heard similar declarations before, including once from a man covered in his dead wife's blood.

"I know you don't understand that. I hope you never do. I was sick. I had a sick way of relating with people I love."

"Did you ever hit Melissa?" Aaron dreaded the answer to his question. Melissa had told him her father had never hit her, but abuse victims sometimes lied, as much to themselves as anyone.

"No." Draper's gaze remained steady, though Aaron could tell it took effort for the man to look him in the eye. "There wasn't a sexual element with her, you see, like there was with her mother. That made the difference. Because of what happened to me. I was punishing Karen for what she made me·feel."

Before Aaron could respond, movement at the front of

the house caught his attention. He spotted Melissa running toward his truck.

He ran toward her, instantly on alert. Had something happened inside? "Melissa!"

She whirled around to look at him, her eyes bright with unshed tears. Her gaze slid past him toward her father, who caught up as Aaron slowed to a jog near the truck.

"I can't talk to you right now," she said to her father. "Maybe later, but not now."

Aaron was a little surprised Draper didn't try to convince her to go back inside. He glanced toward the house and saw Karen Draper standing in the doorway, watching them. She held something blue clutched in her hand. When she dabbed her eyes with it, he realized it was a napkin.

"I don't think Karen would have told my story," Draper said softly as Melissa shut herself inside the truck cab. "You keep it to yourself, too. I'll tell her about it when she's ready to listen."

Aaron looked back at Draper, not sure how he felt about the man now. He couldn't forget what Melissa had told him about her life under the constant threat of her father's violent temper, but he found himself believing Draper when he said that he had changed fundamentally since then.

But it didn't really matter what he thought, did it?

The only thing that mattered was what Melissa believed.

He pulled his keys from his pocket and started around the truck. Derek Draper called his name, stopping him.

"I always liked you, Aaron. Even when you were hell-raising." Draper's gaze drifted toward the truck cab, where his daughter sat hunched and self-protective. "She deserves someone who'll love her the right way. She's never had that. So if you're the man I think you are, deep down, treat her right. I want you to promise me that, Aaron. Promise me you'll take good care of her, whatever happens."

Aaron realized if he made a promise to Draper, he'd have to keep it. He'd spent his twenty-nine years of life avoiding such vows. Avoiding the trappings—and traps—of commitment.

He and Melissa weren't a couple. He didn't even know how he felt about the idea, despite his attraction to her. He certainly didn't know how she felt about him; sometimes he thought she could barely tolerate him.

But Draper was right about one thing. Melissa deserved to be treated better than she ever had been in her short life. And the one thing he knew he could promise was to protect her from whoever wanted her dead.

"I'll take care of her," he told her father. "I promise."

Draper gave a satisfied nod and started walking up the flagstone path toward his waiting wife.

Aaron rounded the truck and slid behind the steering wheel. As he buckled up he glanced at Melissa, who sat stiffly in the passenger seat, her hands twined tightly in her lap.

"I don't want to talk," she said as he started to speak.

He fell quiet, starting the truck's engine. The radio filled the silence in the cab, jarringly loud. He reached out to shut it off, but Melissa grabbed his hand.

"Leave it on," she said, releasing his hand.

They drove home in the gathering darkness, the headlights slicing the night like a knife.

MELISSA WOKE to the smell of bacon frying. Blinking away the sleep in her eyes, she dragged herself out of bed and into her bathrobe, padding barefoot out of the bedroom. She found Aaron at the stove, Jasper sitting obediently at his heel.

"You hungry?" Aaron asked without turning around.

"You talking to me or the dog?"

He glanced over his shoulder at her. "You. I know Jasper's hungry. He stays hungry. Don't you boy?"

Jasper wagged his tail happily, but remained seated.

Melissa frowned at the puppy. How was Aaron managing to keep him so calm? Usually when she was cooking, Jasper danced and jumped around her begging for his portion. Sometimes she had to close him out of the kitchen until she was finished.

"You're being such a good boy, Jasper," she crooned.

The puppy spared her a glance before gazing back up at Aaron, an adoring expression on his fuzzy face.

"The secret to a well-behaved puppy," Aaron murmured, flipping bacon in the skillet, "is plenty of exercise. I took him out for a run this morning. Five miles, full throttle."

"Oh, so that's what I've been doing wrong." She grimaced at the thought of a five mile run every morning. She was too clumsy to be much of a runner. She tried to get in a long walk every day, but usually without Jasper, who had too much energy to put up with the slower pace. "I've been planning to fence in the back when he gets older and I feel like I can leave him outside by himself for any length of time."

Aaron transferred the bacon onto a stack of folded paper towels to drain. "Scrambled eggs okay with you?"

She settled into a dining room chair to watch him cook. "Sure. I could go for eggs."

"Anything to keep from talking about last night?"

Her stomach knotted, turning the hunger rumbles in her belly into queasiness. "Not much to talk about."

"Did you believe what your mother told you?" he asked.

She'd finally talked to him a little bit last night once they made it back to the cottage. He'd shared what she suspected was a condensed version of what her father had told him, which had concurred with her mother's version, but he'd been kind enough not to push her into a longer dissection of the visit to her parents' house.

Apparently his patience had run out.

"I don't know," she answered, crossing her arms protectively over her aching stomach. "I want to."

"Do you?" Aaron set aside the bowl of eggs he'd been mixing and turned to look at her. "Or is it easier to keep thinking he's the same old liar?"

She wanted to argue, but Aaron had a point. Letting herself believe her father had changed, after all this time, was just setting herself up for disappointment if it turned out to be another deception.

"My mother said he's completely different now." She ran her fingernail over a nick in the wood table. "*She's* completely different now. She has been for a while. I noticed it before, but I thought she was putting on a show so I wouldn't worry."

"I talked to your mother on the phone last night," Aaron said. "She gave me the name of the clinic. This morning I talked to his counselor, with your father's permission."

She frowned. "You shouldn't have involved yourself, Aaron. It's not your problem."

He frowned back at her. "I knew you wouldn't do it."

"Which is my right."

He blew out a long breath. "You're right. I stepped over the line. I'm sorry."

She couldn't be angry with him. She knew he was only trying to help her. "What did the counselor say?"

"That your father has worked hard to change his behavior. He apparently goes back every week to see the counselor, even now. Your parents also get unscheduled visits from a social services caseworker once or twice a month, just to monitor how things are going with them."

Melissa couldn't believe what she was hearing. "There's no way my father would have agreed to such a thing."

"According to the counselor, your father insisted on it." Aaron turned back to the eggs, pouring them into the hot skillet. "I know I'm not an expert on human behavior or anything, but I'm pretty good at reading whether or not a perp is lying to me, you know?"

"And what did you think of what my father told you?"

Aaron stirred the eggs, not answering immediately.

She watched the muscles of his arm flex and bunch as he scrambled the eggs until they were fluffy, acutely aware of how he filled the small kitchen with his enormous presence. There was a part of her that wanted to wrap herself in his strength, to let him shield her from all threats. But she couldn't think that way. She couldn't depend on anyone else for anything.

Aaron remained silent as he spooned the eggs onto two plates, added slices of bacon to each and carried both to the table where she sat. He slid one plate in front of her. "I believed him."

Melissa looked down at the food, certain she wouldn't be able to keep any of it down. "And I believed my mother."

Aaron settled in the chair next to her. "That's enough for now. Don't you think?"

She looked up at him. "You mean I don't have to go running over there to talk to them today?" She managed a wry smile. "That's what they'd do on a TV show."

He smiled back, closing his fingers around hers. "They've worked on the problem that drove you away from your family. Good for them. But that doesn't mean the damage just goes away. You deal with the situation however you wish. If that means you need more time, then take more time."

A muted trill kept her from having to respond through the lump in her throat. It was her cell phone, and based on the ring tone it was someone from the office.

With a little cough to clear her throat, she pulled her hand from Aaron's and crossed to the sofa, where she'd left her purse. "This is Melissa," she answered.

"Whew—wasn't sure I'd get you." Dalton Brant sounded relieved on the other end of the line. "Didn't know if you were keeping your phone on during your…vacation."

She didn't miss the snide tone at the end of the sentence. She sighed. "What can I do for you, Dalton?"

"Carter called—he needs the Thomas contract file from last fall, and I can't find it anywhere. I hoped you had a copy."

She did, but it was in the file cabinet at home. "It's at my house. I could get it and run it by the office."

"Oh, that would be great!" The snide tone in Dalton's voice was gone, eclipsed by palpable relief. "You don't know how I was freaking out when I couldn't find the file copy."

"We still need to figure out where that went," Melissa reminded him.

"I called Alice to see if she knew, but she didn't answer."

"She's on vacation."

"I know that." The snide tone was back.

Melissa sighed. "I'll be there in about an hour with the copy. Hang tight." She hung up and turned to Aaron. "I've got to get a file from home and take it to the office."

"Okay. I'll come with you."

Knowing it would be pointless to argue with him, she gave a nod and headed for the bedroom to dress.

"YOU'RE GOING to regret missing breakfast," Aaron warned later as she emerged from the hallway fully dressed. She hadn't eaten anything he'd prepared, though he'd taken time to wolf down his own portion before she finished dressing.

"I'll eat a good lunch, I promise," she said, glancing at her watch. "I hope I can find the file quickly—I promised

Dalton I'd be there in an hour, and thirty minutes of that are already gone."

"He'll deal," Aaron said flatly, wondering why she even cared. It wasn't like that Brant jerk was nice to her in the first place. "He's probably the one who lost the original contract in the first place."

"He doesn't do the filing. Alice does. Since she's on vacation this week, he couldn't ask her about it. She probably just filed it somewhere Dalton wasn't expecting."

He pulled onto Tuckahaw Road, heading east toward her house. "Have you even had a chance to talk to your insurance agent about the repairs?"

"He went by the house to do an assessment the same day it happened," she answered. "He's scheduled a crew to get to work later this week." She looked at him, a little furrow in her brow. "I need to find somewhere to stay besides the cottage."

"You don't like it there?" He felt a twinge of dismay.

"I love it there, but I can't put your family out forever."

"Mom told me you're welcome to stay until your house repairs are done." He slowed and turned left into Melissa's drive.

He walked around to her side to open the door. She stumbled as she got out, missing her footing, and pitched forward toward him. He wrapped his arms around her to keep her from falling.

She clutched his upper arms, her fingers digging into his flesh. In an instant, his body reacted to the unexpected feel of her breasts flattened against his chest. Her warm breath washed across his neck, stoking the simmer of fire in his blood until he felt as if his whole body was ablaze.

Melissa gazed up at him with stunned eyes, color flooding her cheeks. Her eyes darkened, her gaze fluttering down to settle on his mouth.

His breath hitched, trapped somewhere deep in his lungs. He bent toward her, his own gaze fixed on the Cupid's bow curve of her pink lips. Trembling, they parted and a soft, sweet breath kissed his lips with a hint of mint toothpaste.

Oh, he wanted to taste her. He wanted it more than he wanted his next breath.

In the distance, a dog barked. Melissa's body twitched, and she stepped away from him. He saw her throat bob nervously as she turned to face the house. "Sorry," she rasped. "I'm such a klutz."

Aching with frustration, he followed her up the sidewalk to the house. As they neared the wooden porch steps, something just in front of the first step glittered in the morning sunlight, catching Aaron's eye. He paused while Melissa went on, trying to make sense of what he was seeing. It looked like a wire—

His heart jumped into his throat. "Stop!"

Melissa jerked to a halt, skidding on loose gravel near the edge of the sidewalk. She teetered, starting to fall forward toward the porch steps.

Aaron leapt forward and grabbed her, crushing her back against his chest. She twisted in his grip, staring up at him with startled blue eyes.

He dragged his gaze away, looking back at the wire he now clearly saw protruding across the bottom of the first step. "That," he said, "is a trip wire."

Melissa twisted in his grasp to follow his gaze. "What?"

He swallowed hard, moving slowly back from the house. "Melissa, I think there's a bomb somewhere around your porch."

Chapter Eleven

Aaron's words rang in Melissa's head, keeping rhythm with her hurtling pulse. *A bomb a bomb a bomb*—

Aaron tugged her backward, but her feet seemed frozen to the sidewalk. He finally dragged her a few steps, his grip so tight she wasn't sure she could breathe. "I want you to go to the truck and stay there. Okay?"

She managed to keep her balance when he let her go. "What are you going to do?"

"Take a closer look."

Her heart jumped in her chest. "Are you crazy?"

"I'm not going to touch it. I just want a closer look."

Fear rattled her bones. "You could trip a wire—"

"I've done this before." He caught her arms in his big hands, making her focus on him. "Go wait in the truck."

"Just in case you do get blown up?" Shivers set in now, her initial shock made worse by the chill morning air.

His lips curved slightly. "I'll do my damnedest to avoid that, I promise." He gave her a nudge toward the truck.

She turned and headed back to the vehicle, her knees trembling. She climbed into the truck cab and gazed through the windshield at Aaron, who walked slowly back to the porch. He stopped right in front of the steps, crouching to get a closer look at what he'd seen.

Please God, please God, please God…

Finally he stood again, striding quickly toward the truck. She released a shaky sigh when he climbed in on the driver's side.

"Is it a bomb?" she asked, her tongue thick in her mouth.

"I think so. The wire seems to be connected to a detonator. If you'd put so much as a toe on that wire, it might have gone off. It looks like it's attached to a pipe bomb hidden in the stoneware urn that sits there by the porch railing but I didn't risk getting close enough to tell for sure." He reached for the police radio attached to the dashboard and called it in.

"Should we be getting the hell out of here?" she asked when he was finished on the radio.

"If it's a pipe bomb, we're safe enough here."

"And if it's not?"

He looked over at her, his brow furrowed. "Good point." He started the truck and reversed quickly out of the drive, pausing only long enough to make sure he wasn't pulling into oncoming traffic.

A mile down the road, he pulled down a dirt turnoff and parked. By the time he cut the engine and called in their new position, Melissa was shaking so hard her teeth rattled.

"Why is this happening?" She couldn't wrap her mind around the idea that someone wanted her dead so much that he'd set a bomb to make it happen.

"I'm going to bring Dalton Brant in and ask him that very question." Aaron's tone was grim and determined.

Melissa's heart sank. She hadn't given a thought to the odd timing of Dalton's call. "That's crazy. I mean, Dalton is snide and jealous, and yeah, he'd stab me in the back figuratively in a heartbeat. But murder? That's just—"

"I know. Crazy." Aaron's thumbs beat a rapid cadence against the steering wheel. His eyes were hooded and intense, the force of his gaze sending a shock through her system. He unbuckled his seat belt, already moving toward her, his eyes locked with hers. She felt his hand unlatch her own belt and had only a second to brace herself before he entwined his fingers in her hair and pulled her into his arms.

His mouth covered hers, and the world seemed to slide out from beneath her feet, plunging her into a void filled with a tangle of sensations—his breath, hot in her mouth as her lips trembled apart, his big hand sliding through her hair and down to cradle her neck as he deepened the kiss. His tongue, hot and wet against hers, coaxed fire into her belly and she closed her fingers around his wrists, holding on for dear life.

The fierce heat of his kiss died down to a warm glow, his lips easing from hers to trace a warm, tingling path over the curve of her jaw. A tiny voice in the back of her head shouted warnings, but she ignored them as easily as she'd ignore the distant buzz of a fly.

She let go of his arms and dropped her hands to his body, tracing the sloping line from his broad chest to his narrower waist under the edges of his leather jacket. His body was hot and hard muscled through the layer of cotton separating her fingers from his skin, confirming what she'd observed with her eyes—he was as fit now as he'd been during his playing days.

He was the one who finally pulled away, easing her hands away from his sides and holding them between his own hands as he sat back and looked at her through slightly narrowed eyes.

"I shouldn't have done that," he said. But he didn't sound sorry.

"Probably not," she agreed, her voice a breathless rasp. Her rational side roared back with a vengeance and she tugged her hands from his, turning to face the front of the truck. "You can pretend it didn't happen if you want."

"What if I don't want to?"

She darted a quick look at him. He was watching her, his eyes the color of storm clouds. "Aaron—"

She stopped as she heard the sound of approaching sirens. Within a few seconds a pair of Chickasaw County Sheriff's Department cruisers passed their position at the turnoff, followed by a fire truck rumbling up Tuckahaw Road behind the deputies. A third cruiser slowed at the turnoff and pulled in next to them. Riley Patterson sat behind the wheel. He parked the cruiser and unfolded himself from the driver's seat, crossing to Aaron's side of the truck.

Aaron lowered the window. "I think it's a pipe bomb with a trip wire attached to some sort of detonator. The bomb's in the stoneware urn at the top of the steps."

"Bennett's taking a look," Riley answered, nodding toward the cruisers that had passed moments before. "He was part of an Army EOD team a few years back," he told Melissa.

"Explosive Ordnance Disposal," Aaron added for her benefit. "He's our go-to guy on bombs."

Thumbing the call button on the cruiser's radio, Riley called in the bomb's location to Bennett, then turned back to Aaron and Melissa. "We've already sent a request that the Borland Police Department pick up Dalton Brant for questioning. We're supposed to get a call when they have him in custody."

Melissa shook her head. "I don't believe he'd set a bomb at my house. It has to be a coincidence. I mean I've had to supply copies of files from my home office before, so it's not unprecedented—"

"We'll give him a chance to account for his whereabouts."

She wrapped her jacket tightly around her, trying not to let her teeth chatter. "Nobody's been to my house in a couple of days. Anyone could have set up the booby-trap within that time. How will he possibly be able to account for his whereabouts for the last forty-eight hours?"

"That's for Brant to worry about, not you." Aaron reached into the backseat of the truck's crew cab, pulled out a folded fleece blanket stored there and handed it to Melissa. "Bundle up. You're shivering."

Though his words were brisk and businesslike, she didn't miss the gentle warmth in his gray eyes. Had it been only a few moments ago that he'd held her so close she'd felt as if she was part of him? She could still feel the heat of his mouth on hers, the smell of his shave lotion lingering on her clothes.

Shivering, though not from cold, she took the blanket and wrapped it over herself, glad for the extra warmth.

"You should probably get her out of here," Riley suggested. "Somebody could have set the bomb as a distraction. I'm going to give you a sirens-on escort to the main highway, just in case somebody's thinking about an ambush."

As Riley returned to the cruiser, Melissa turned to stare at Aaron. "I can't believe he seriously thinks someone might be lying in wait for us."

"He's just taking precautions," Aaron assured her. "I don't think whoever's behind these attempts is going to set up any kind of attack in the open. These are sneak attacks. He won't risk getting caught in the act."

"You really think it's Dalton."

"The timing of his call is suspicious."

"He could have had anyone else in the office make the call for him, if he was trying not to incriminate himself. Why wouldn't he?" she asked.

"That's one of the things I'd like to ask him." Aaron started the truck and followed Riley's wailing cruiser onto Tuckahaw Road.

"SOMEONE SET A BOMB at Melissa's house?" Dalton Brant looked from Riley to Aaron, his face growing increasingly pale. "And you think I know something about it?"

Aaron remained silent, letting Riley direct the interview for the moment. He was still technically on vacation; he didn't want to do anything to get crossways with his captain.

"Can you account for your whereabouts for the last forty-eight hours?" Riley asked, his voice carefully neutral. Brant knew his legal rights. Flinging any sort of accusations would only ensure that he clammed up.

"Am I a suspect?"

"We're actually trying to eliminate you," Riley said reasonably. "Since you were the one who called Ms. Draper about the contract file, you're the first person we need to cross off our list. Once we show you can't be the one who set the bomb, it'll free us to go after more plausible suspects."

Brant's wide brow creased as he narrowed his eyes at Riley. "I'm not sure why a call to a colleague about a contract she was part of drafting makes me a person of interest in the first place."

"Just procedure. We don't want a homicidal bomber to go free because we didn't cover all our bases." Riley's placid smile was carefully designed to put Brant at ease.

Brant eyed Aaron. "Why aren't you looking at the loser husbands of her pro bono clients? Aren't they more likely to be your mad bomber than someone like me?"

"We're looking at them as well," Aaron lied. For now he wasn't looking at them at all, thanks to Melissa's plea that he spare her clients any unnecessary stress.

But if Brant didn't break and incriminate himself, he'd have to renegotiate his deal with Melissa. He understood her concerns, but he couldn't let her sacrifice her own safety to protect a client's peace of mind.

"Is Melissa okay?" Brant asked suddenly.

"She's fine," Aaron answered shortly. At least she had been when he left her at the marina with his parents and, in a stroke of luck, his sister-in-law Kristen, a Gossamer Ridge police detective. She was off duty that day and with his niece, Maddy, in school and his brother, Sam, at work in Birmingham she'd been free to play bodyguard for Melissa, allowing Aaron to sit in on Dalton Brant's interview.

"I guess she's probably told you we've had our differences at work," Brant said carefully. "She's the boss's pet."

"And that bugs you?" Aaron sat back, his hands folded over his flat stomach. "You're Harvard educated, right?"

Brant's left eyebrow twitched upward. "You've done a background check on me?"

"Nah, the Borland detectives noticed the diploma on your cubicle wall when they picked you up," Aaron answered.

"Oh." Brant flashed a weak, sheepish smile. "Yeah. Harvard Law."

"I'd have thought you'd stay up north somewhere, maybe New York or D.C., instead of coming back here to Podunkville," Riley commented.

"My family was from here. My girlfriend at the time."

"Why did you need the contract you sent Melissa to find?"

"Actually, it was Carter who needed it," Brant answered. "He has a meeting later this afternoon with the client in question and he wanted to have the contract with him."

"Is that unusual?" Riley asked.

"Not really." Brant shrugged. "What's unusual is not being able to find a copy of the file in the office."

"You still haven't located it?"

"We've been trying to contact our office assistant, Alice Gaines, who does most of the filing. Maybe she filed it somewhere besides the obvious. But she's on vacation and nobody's been able to reach her on her cell." Brant's brow accordioned. "It's not like her not to call us back, though. I wonder if she went on a cruise or something."

Aaron made a mental note to find out. It wasn't likely that the office assistant had a motive to want Melissa dead, but her absence just at the time of the attacks could be used by a good defense attorney to cast reasonable doubt if they hadn't done their homework.

The last thing he wanted was for the person tormenting Melissa to go unpunished because the Chickasaw County Sheriff's Department hadn't closed all the possible gaps in the case.

"SO RILEY'S interviewing the suspect right now?" Kristen Cooper handed Melissa a cup of steaming coffee and settled in the armchair across from her, setting her own cup on a corkwood coaster on the oak coffee table between them.

"I think so." Melissa wrapped her hands around the mug, grateful for the warmth. Outside, storm clouds scudded across the sky to the west, sending the temperatures plunging into the high thirties as sunset approached. A light rain had begun to fall around three o'clock, sending a flurry of fishermen off the lake for the day and freeing Hannah and her sister-in-law, Mariah, to knock off work early and join Kristen and Melissa in the cozy living room of the guest cottage.

Hannah had been watching Jasper for Melissa, so she'd brought the puppy along and now sat in an adjacent armchair, the puppy curled up in her lap. Hannah's son, Cody, was napping in a portable playpen in the bedroom nearest the living room, the door open so they could hear if he woke.

Mariah was Aaron's other sister-in-law, a slim, fashion-model gorgeous woman in her mid-twenties with rich olive skin and eyes the color of quicksilver. She was married to Aaron's brother Jake. Kristen was married to Sam, a Jefferson County prosecutor Melissa had heard of but never met. She was a little shorter and less statuesque than Mariah, with kittenish features, honey-blond hair and bright blue eyes.

Melissa liked them both, she decided within minutes of meeting them. Mariah was a sweetheart, with a kind spirit and gentle empathy, while Kristen had a no-nonsense attitude that made Melissa feel as if there was a real chance she could find a way to make sense of the insanity that had overtaken her life in the last few days.

"You hear about normal guys just cracking every now and then," Hannah said. "Maybe this Dalton Brant guy is like that."

"But even those guys have some sort of motive, like losing their jobs or breaking up with their wives or girlfriends," Melissa insisted. "Getting ticked off because I get a few extra bucks in my paycheck than he does? I'm sorry. I don't buy that. I'm not even close to the top of the pay scale at the office. Why not go after someone who makes serious money, if it's about professional jealousy?"

"Some people don't need a reason to kill." There was a dark undertone to Mariah's voice that caught Melissa by surprise.

"Ted Bundy seemed pretty normal to most people who knew him," Hannah said.

"Let's say it's not Dalton," Kristen suggested. "What about the rest of the people you work with? Anybody else seem a little hinky to you?"

Melissa laughed softly. "I'd probably be the most hinky person in the office. Pushing thirty, never married, haven't dated in years—"

She almost added, "haven't been kissed since law school," but stopped. That wasn't true anymore, thanks to Aaron's bone-shattering kiss in the truck earlier that day.

She'd spent the last few hours trying not to think about what had happened between her and Aaron after they discovered the bomb, afraid she'd make it out to be more than it was—a simple physical response to the danger they'd just survived. Based on the way Aaron had slipped right into cop mode and left her behind at the marina with barely a goodbye, he hadn't seen it as anything more and neither should she.

She cleared her throat. "Believe me, if Jasper were a dozen cats instead of one dog, I'd be a cliché."

Hannah laughed gently, and even Kristen cracked a smile. But Mariah's gaze was serious. She leaned over and put her hand on Melissa's hand. "I don't think you're hinky."

Melissa smiled at her. "Thank you."

"Every place I've ever worked, there were dramas to sort through," Kristen said. "Even at the cop shop. Like the time we all started to suspect that Officer Davenport was cheating on his wife with one of the nurses at County—"

"He was," Hannah said flatly. "The dog."

Melissa frowned. "You mean, is something like that going on at the firm?"

"You have how many people working there?"

"Eight. Six lawyers, two support staffers." Melissa sighed. "But I don't gossip."

"This isn't gossip," Kristen said firmly. "This is trying to figure out whether or not anybody in your office had something to hide, something big enough to kill for."

Melissa shook her head. "Who's going to kill over an affair? Everybody at the office knows I don't get involved in their personal dramas."

"But there was an affair?" Kristen prodded.

"I don't know." She had been trying not to think about what she'd seen a week ago, mostly because it involved her boss, Carter, who had a perfectly lovely wife and three beautiful, successful, grown children. "It could be nothing."

"You don't have to tell me who. Just tell me what," Kristen suggested.

Melissa licked her lips, feeling guilty. Even if she was right, and Carter was having an affair, he wouldn't try to kill her just because she'd run into the two of them together after work hours. "I was in Birmingham last weekend meeting a client to draw up a contract. I stayed in town for dinner and ran into another lawyer from my office having dinner with one of our support staff. He said he'd just run into her—"

"In Birmingham?" Hannah looked skeptical.

Melissa sighed. "I know. It looked bad. But maybe it really happened that way. The woman—let's call her Ann—was going on vacation, so she might have been in Birmingham to catch a red-eye flight or something."

"You don't know where she was going?"

Melissa shook her head. "Nobody seems to know. A— Ann is a pretty private person. Never seemed to be into drama, either."

"And you never suspected anything between this Ann person and the other lawyer before?"

"No. But like I said, I wasn't really paying a lot of attention to those sorts of undercurrents at the office." Melissa didn't add that she kept a low profile because she didn't want her coworkers asking a lot of questions about her own life. Or lack of one.

"So you saw the other lawyer with Ann—he's married, I assume?" Kristen asked.

"Yes."

"Do you know his wife?"

"Barely. She comes to the office Christmas party, so we've met a few times. But we're not friends."

Kristen frowned, her expression thoughtful. "You're right. Your lawyer friend probably knows you wouldn't tell his wife anything. You're not a gossip, so you're not going to be spilling his business to anyone else at the office. He wouldn't see it as a reason to target you."

Though she hadn't really thought of Carter as a potential suspect, she was glad to have Kristen mark him off the list of possible suspects, anyway.

She just hoped Aaron and Riley were marking Dalton off their suspect list as well.

"I HATE TO SAY IT, but so far all his alibis are checking out," Riley told Aaron later that afternoon. It hadn't taken Dalton Brant long to realize he needed to shut up and lawyer up. Nor was it a surprise that he'd called in one of the top criminal lawyers in Alabama, who'd forced the deputies to concede they had no evidence to hold his client any longer.

Brant had already outlined his whereabouts for the last two days, and Riley and Aaron had been making calls to check his story since. Brant's girlfriend gave him an alibi for the last two evenings, and his work associates all vouched for his presence in the office for most of his ten-hour work days.

"The timing of his call to Melissa could just be a coincidence. That bomb could have been waiting there since the morning after the fire, in hopes Melissa would return for more clothes or something," Riley pointed out.

Aaron didn't want to give up on Dalton Brant as a suspect yet, but the man had all his bases covered. He couldn't have been the one who planted the bomb. He wouldn't have had the opportunity.

But anyone might have had the means, it turned out. Mitch Bennett entered the bullpen a few minutes later, his expression somewhere between grim and self-satisfied. "Got the details on the bomb." He handed a file folder to Aaron.

Aaron looked it over quickly. Run of the mill pipe bomb, loaded with nails and ball bearings for shrapnel when it went off. The trip wire had been attached to an electronic detonator designed to switch on once the wire moved forward.

"The perp could have bought the detonator components at any number of electronics stores in the area," Bennett said. "God knows, you can find directions for making the damned thing online so just about anyone could've done it. At least we have all the components intact. We're lucky it didn't blow."

Aaron grimaced. "You think *you're* lucky."

Bennett flashed him a grim smile. "Point taken. Anyway, we're going to start piecing together all the parts and see if I can track down where they came from. I have a friend at the local ATF office who'll be interested in this nasty little puzzle. I'll call you as soon as I know anything."

Riley clapped Aaron on the shoulder. "I know you're going to want to stay here all night and hammer away at the case, but there's not much we can do right now until Bennett and his pals finish going over that bomb for evidence. Besides, you're on vacation, remember? I'm betting Melissa's probably chomping at the bit for an update, too."

Aaron nodded, although facing Melissa was going to be a little more complicated than Riley knew. She'd been awfully quiet on the drive to the marina after the bomb scare, apparently in no mood to discuss the kiss they'd shared moments before. Knowing her past history with men, he didn't blame her for extreme caution and he hadn't pushed her to talk for fear of scaring her away.

But now he wondered if she was going to ignore the kiss altogether.

As he shrugged on his coat, the phone on Riley's desk

rang. Riley grabbed it, listening for a moment. His brow furrowed and he looked up at Aaron, his expression grim.

His stomach knotting, Aaron waited for Riley to hang up. "What is it?"

"Another bomb," Riley answered, his tone hard and angry. "And this time, somebody got hurt."

Chapter Twelve

The house on Shelby Avenue would have been easy to locate even without the phalanx of rescue vehicles and police cruisers lining the narrow road in front of the one-story bungalow. Attendants were loading someone on a gurney into the back of an ambulance when Aaron got out of his truck, catching up with Riley, who'd arrived in one of the Sheriff's Department cruisers. They went in search of Blake Clayton, who'd been first on the scene.

Aaron's heart dropped as he recognized what was left of the pockmarked porch, which had sustained the worst damage from the blast. He'd been here just yesterday with Melissa, to pick up her puppy from the dog-sitter. What was the woman's name?

"Amy DeLong," Blake supplied before Aaron could ask. "She got off easier than she might have. The raccoon took the brunt of the blast." He nodded toward a plastic garbage bag sitting on the ground by the police cruiser. "Apparently the poor critter wandered up looking for food and hit a trip wire connected to the bomb. It was under the porch steps."

"How about Amy DeLong? Was that her in the ambulance?" Aaron asked.

"Like I said, she was lucky. She was just inside when it blew, but the door is pretty solid and kept out the nails and screws the bastard used to pack the pipe bomb. The glass in the door blew in, though, and she caught some pretty nasty cuts from that. Part of the pipe hit her in the head, too, knocking her out for a little bit, so the paramedics are taking her to the hospital in Gossamer Ridge to observe her overnight. She looks like she'll be okay, though."

"Thank God," Riley said.

Aaron pulled his brother-in-law aside, lowering his voice. "Riley, Amy DeLong keeps Melissa's dog when she goes to work."

Riley's eyes widened. "You're kidding me."

Aaron shook his head, his blood like ice. "Somebody really wants her dead."

Riley's expression darkened. "We need to figure out who besides Dalton Brant knew that she would be coming into the office today. He—"

"Or she," Aaron added.

"Or she," Riley conceded, "might have figured Melissa would keep to her normal work routine. They wouldn't know my wife has fallen madly in puppy love and would have paid Melissa for the opportunity to watch the mutt for her."

"I need to call Melissa before she hears about this from somebody else." Aaron stepped away, pulling out his cell phone and dialing the number of the guest house.

Hannah answered, catching him by surprise. "Oh, hey, Skipper. Is Melissa there?"

"Yeah. Is something up? You sound weird."

"I'll explain in a bit. Just let me talk to Melissa a minute." Aaron waited for his sister to pass the phone to Melissa. In the background he heard other voices, one he recognized as his sister-in-law, Kristen. He was relieved to hear her voice, now that Melissa was in more danger than ever.

Melissa came on the line. "What's wrong?"

He didn't try to ease into it, telling her what had happened at Amy DeLong's home earlier that afternoon.

"Oh my God. I need to go see her—"

"No. You need to stay right where you are. I'm heading your way as fast as I can. The EMTs seem to think she's going to be okay. We'll call her hospital room later tonight when she's had a chance to be processed through the E.R." He looked back at the ruins of Amy DeLong's porch, his gut aching. "Let me speak to Kristen a moment, please."

Melissa handed over the phone to Kristen, after murmuring a quick explanation of what was going on. Kristen came on the line, her voice solid and reassuring. "I'm armed and now I'm on alert," she told Aaron without preamble. "I'll be here when you get here. Don't worry."

"Thanks, Kristen."

He hung up and walked back to where Riley was taking notes from Blake Clayton. Riley shot him a quick glance. "Everything okay back at the ranch?"

Aaron nodded. "I'm heading out. Call Hannah soon. She knows what's going on by now, and she'll be worried about you."

Riley smiled. "Will do."

Aaron headed for his truck, sparing one last look at the mangled porch and thanking God he'd spotted the tripwire at Melissa's house in time.

"I KEEP WAITING to wake up." Melissa tightened her grip on the edges of the crocheted throw Aaron had pulled from the hall closet when he'd noticed her shivering. She hadn't the heart to tell him that the cold had less to do with her tremors than the sheer terror of realizing just how relentless—and ruthless—her unknown stalker could be.

Aaron moved from the armchair across from her, settling beside her on the sofa to slide his arm around her shoulders and tuck her close. He was blessedly warm against her side, and she relaxed against him.

"It could have been a lot worse," he said.

"Would have been, if not for the poor raccoon."

"Amy was lucky."

"All this because she's my friend." Her chest tightened with guilt. "Who else will they target—my office?" A horrible thought occurred to her. "Oh, my God, Aaron—my parents—"

"I sent a patrol to your parents' house already," Aaron assured her. "They searched the place for any sign of a bomb or an intruder. I got the all clear just before I got here."

Melissa went limp with relief. However complicated her feelings about her parents might be, she didn't want either of them hurt, especially not because of her.

"We've also contacted the Borland police to pay a visit to your office to check the premises for any sign of sabotage. But I think that's not as likely, especially if someone at the office is behind this."

She shook her head. Her colleagues at the law firm were good people. Nice people. Even Dalton Brant, for all his occasional pettiness, was a decent enough guy when you got down to the basics. How could any of them have tried to kill her?

Why would they even want to?

"This cottage is the safest place for you. It's not easily accessible from the road, and there are always a lot of people around, so it's not easy to get close to this place without being noticed." Aaron lowered his voice, as if sharing a secret with her. "When my brother Sam was trying to protect his daughter from a kidnapper, this is where they stayed."

"I feel safer here than anywhere," she admitted.

He squeezed her shoulder with one large hand, his touch remarkably gentle. "We're getting closer to solving this thing, I promise. Having the first bomb intact is going to give us a lot of good leads to follow."

"It almost has to be someone connected to my office in some way," Melissa said aloud, even though she didn't want to believe it. The bomb at her own house could have been set by anyone who knew where she lived, but the bomb at Amy's house suggested the bomber knew her daily schedule. And since she didn't have many friends outside of work these days, that left her coworkers.

"We can't eliminate other people, including the husbands and boyfriends of the abused women you represent," Aaron pointed out. "Would any of them know your connection to Amy DeLong?"

"Through my clients, maybe," Melissa admitted. "I've picked up Jasper at Amy's house a few times when I was with some of my clients—I've had him for almost five months now and he's been staying with her since he was very little."

"Can you remember which clients?"

She shook her head. "I'm not dragging them into this. Even if they knew where Amy lived, they didn't know her name. They certainly weren't likely to tell the men who abused them anything about her."

"You could have been followed," Aaron argued. "Damn it, Melissa, you could have been killed today if you'd taken just a few more steps up your front walk. Amy DeLong's lucky she isn't dead. How many more close calls before you realize you can't protect these women at the risk of your life?"

She pulled away from him, horribly torn. She knew keeping her client list secret only put her in greater danger. But she'd made these women a promise she couldn't break without thinking long and hard about the possible consequences.

She turned to look at Aaron. "You don't know how hard it is to get some of these women to trust me and my motives."

Aaron pushed to his feet, his gaze flashing fire. "I do

know." He closed the distance between them, catching her face between his large hands. "Believe me, I know."

His gaze ensnared hers, the determination in his gunmetal eyes setting sparks through her rattled nervous system. She wanted to pull away from his touch but found herself unable to move, as if her body itself were rebelling against her weakening will. She closed her eyes, hoping that by shutting out his overpowering gaze she could loosen the fetters holding her pinned in place, but even in the darkness behind her eyelids she couldn't ignore the rough texture of Aaron's thumbs as they slowly, deliberately stroked gentle circles over her cheeks.

"Don't shut me out," he whispered, his breath warm against her lips. "Please."

She opened her eyes to find him closer than ever. One of his hands moved around to the back of her neck, reminding her of that morning in the truck when he'd pulled her to him for that earth-shattering kiss.

Kiss me again, she thought, moving toward him without intending to do so. She was powerless to resist him, a fact which terrified her as much as it enthralled her.

This was so wrong. So risky. After Evan, she'd been so careful about the people she allowed herself to be around.

So careful that you ended up all alone, taunted a voice in her head.

Aaron lowered his head, his movements slow and careful as if consciously giving her the chance to stop him.

She should. She should put her hands up and push him away, before she lost all control of the situation—and herself.

But when she lifted her hands to his chest, her fingers curled in the soft cotton of his shirt, anchoring herself to him as she rose to her tiptoes to meet his descending lips.

Hot. Sweet. Hot again. His hands cradled her face, the

touch remarkably light and tender as if he was afraid she would break without much effort. She ran her hands down his sides, her fingers seeking and finding the ribbed contours of his muscles, hard and hot beneath her touch.

"Melissa," he murmured against her mouth, the word devolving to a groan as she ran her knuckles against the waistband of his jeans.

The sound of the groan hit her system like a bucket of water in the face. She pulled back from him, horrified at how easily she'd let herself fall victim to her own desires again.

She knew, academically, that sex could be a wonderful affirmation of love and devotion. But she and Aaron weren't anywhere near that sort of emotion, were they? They were barely friends, if that.

Nor could she forget Tina Lewis's warning. Aaron had a reputation for short term relationships. Melissa hadn't needed Tina Lewis to tell her that. Chickasaw County was small town Alabama. News traveled faster than traffic on the main highway.

She could pretend she was okay with a no-strings fling with Aaron Cooper. But it would only be a trap. Just as sex with Evan had been a trap, each act of intimacy a set of blinders she'd worn to shut out the reality of who he really was.

Aaron Cooper might not be abusive like Evan or her father. He might be a pretty decent guy.

She just couldn't let herself get close enough to find out.

"I'm sorry," Aaron said quietly. "I shouldn't have—surprised you that way."

She gave a small huff of mortified laughter. "It's no problem. We're just both keyed up." She started to move past him, toward the bedroom.

He caught her arm, his grip gentle but firm. "It's not about being keyed up."

She forced herself to meet his gaze without wavering. "That's as good an excuse as any."

Aaron's eyes narrowed. "So we just ignore what's going on between us? Pretend it's not there?"

"I think we shouldn't let it be a big deal," she clarified. "You're a man. I'm a woman. We have a little chemistry. Doesn't mean it's a good idea to do anything about it."

"You're interested in someone else."

She couldn't hold back a laugh. "No."

"Then what is it?" He almost looked hurt.

"You said yourself you don't do the girlfriend thing."

He looked defensive. "I know what I told you."

"We're not suited."

His eyebrows notched upward. "That felt pretty suitable."

"Sexual attraction isn't the basis of a relationship."

"It's not a bad place to start," Aaron said with a little grin that made her heart flip. She felt her defenses crumbling all over again.

Fortunately, Aaron took a step back, crossing his arms over his chest. "Okay, I get the message. I'm going to check with Riley before I head to bed, but you go on. You look beat."

She hid a frown as she headed for the bedroom, trying not to be stung by his sudden detachment. It was what she wanted, wasn't it? She'd been the one to put a stop to their kiss. She was the one who'd made it clear she wasn't interested in anything more with him.

So why did she feel as if she'd been kicked in the teeth?

RILEY HAD ALREADY left the office by the time Aaron called, so he tried his home number. Hannah answered. "I thought you might call. How's Melissa holding up?"

"Stressed." He didn't want to talk about Melissa. Right now he didn't have time to deal with her mood shifts.

He was too busy saving her pretty little butt.

"Riley checked with the hospital—Amy DeLong is going to be fine. Her cuts were minor, and the doctors think her concussion is as well. They plan to release her tomorrow."

"Good news," Aaron agreed, realizing he forgot to call the hospital to check on Amy as he'd promised Melissa they would. He made a mental note to give her an update on her friend's condition before he went to bed. "Skipper, I need to talk to Riley for a minute, okay?"

Riley sounded tired over the phone line. "How'd I know I'd hear from you again before the night was done?"

"Because you'd be calling me if the situation was reversed?" Aaron countered.

"I don't have anything new for you yet. It's only been a couple of hours."

"I know. But I had a couple of new thoughts. We still haven't heard from Evan Hallman's parole officer, have we?"

"Not as of this afternoon, no."

"Maybe we should make another call tomorrow. If Hallman's gone AWOL from North Carolina, he might be another pretty damned good person of interest."

"I still think the law office connection is stronger," Riley said. "Or the list of violent, abusive bastards who probably hate Melissa's guts for taking away their favorite punching bags."

"That was my other thought." Aaron told Riley about his earlier discussion with Melissa regarding her pro bono cases. "If one of her clients' abusers tracked her normal routine at any point over the past three or four months, he'd know she took her dog to Amy DeLong's house every day."

"Any chance she'll give us some names?"

"I'm still working on Melissa."

"Well, let me know if she spills anything to you." Riley made a noise that sounded like a yawn.

"Man, you sound worn out. Go get some shut-eye," Aaron suggested. "We can hit the ground running again tomorrow." He hung up, snapping his cell phone closed.

"You're working on me? How, exactly?"

Melissa's voice behind him made his whole body jerk. She stood in the living room entryway, wrapped in a fluffy robe, her eyes flashing electric blue sparks. Released from its tight ponytail, her hair fell in a sleek black waterfall over her shoulders. If he'd wanted to stay mad at her for her obstinacy, he couldn't have managed it. Standing there unadorned and angry as hell, she was pure temptation.

He was beginning to think he even craved her.

"Using my considerable masculine charms, of course," he said with deliberate lightness even though his insides felt twisted into a hot, painful tangle.

"Is that what it's called these days?"

He took a step closer, knowing he shouldn't. But he couldn't stop himself. "If you think what happened here earlier had anything to do with my investigation—"

Her chin came up. "Didn't it?"

He saw her eyes darken, her pupils dilating as he moved another step closer. He smiled, knowing that it wasn't anger fueling that physical response. "It did not."

Her mouth trembled open. "Aaron, I said—"

"I know what you said." He took one final step toward her, stopping within inches. He looked down at her. "And you're right. I don't exactly have a reputation for being a forever kind of guy. I earned it fair and square. But I don't think I'm that guy anymore."

Something in her expression flickered. He couldn't quite read the emotion, but she didn't turn away so he pressed on.

"Maybe I don't know who I am yet. Maybe I need your help finding out. But I know who I'm not. I'm not Evan Hallman. Or your dad. Can't you trust me for that, at least?"

"I don't know," she admitted. "I don't know if I will ever trust anyone again."

He understood her, better than she knew. He knew what it was like to have your world upended, to have friends you thought you'd have for life turn their backs on you once you couldn't get them fifty-yard-line tickets or skybox passes anymore. What he'd been through with the knee injury and the end of his pro football dream hadn't been nearly as traumatic as what Melissa had been through, of course, but those fair-weather friends had betrayed him, left him in the lurch when he needed them the most. He'd been lucky enough to have family to hold his hand when he needed it—and kick his butt when he started feeling too sorry for himself.

Who had been there for Melissa?

Her expression softened, as if she was reading his thoughts. "I'm sorry. I know it's not fair to you."

"Not much about this situation is fair," he agreed. "But I understand better than you think."

Her eyes narrowed with skepticism.

"My brother J.D. was madly in love once. He thought he'd be with Brenda forever. And then, poof. She was gone. One day to the next." It had been the first time someone close to Aaron had died. He'd been eighteen. Watching what losing her had done to his eldest brother had scarred him. "Then Sam fell in love with a woman who loved her career more than she loved him or their daughter. He'd thought their marriage would be forever, too. And then there was Renee." He took a deep breath, realizing he'd never even told his family about Renee.

"Renee?"

"She was someone I knew in college. Someone I thought I loved. I don't know, maybe I did." He had thought so, at the time. He'd been willing to become a one-woman man for her.

"What happened?"

He kept his voice light, even though the memory still had the power to sting. "Blew out my knee and suddenly went from surefire pro football star to a broken-down has-been. She took one look at my new future and went for a different option. So much for happily ever after."

"And now you think nothing is forever." She sounded as if she understood.

He paced away from her, slumping into the arm chair near the fireplace. "That's how it looks, doesn't it?"

Melissa crossed slowly to the sofa, sitting to face him, her gentle gaze warming him more than the dying embers. "You'd be hard to walk away from, I think. Maybe you should consider giving a more deserving woman a chance."

"The way you're giving me a chance?" he countered.

Her expression shuttered immediately. "That's different. But there is something I *can* give you." She pulled a piece of paper from the pocket of her robe and handed it to him.

"What's this?" he asked, unfolding the sheet to find names and phone numbers written there.

"My pro bono clients," she answered. "If you need to talk to them, talk to them." She lifted her gaze, her blue eyes meeting his with resolve. "I trust you to do the right thing."

Aaron held her gaze, aware just how much her admission meant. Maybe she couldn't trust him emotionally. Maybe she was smart not to—he was hardly a safe bet. But trusting him with her clients' secrets was one hell of a start.

He silently promised he'd do everything he could to live up to her faith in him.

Chapter Thirteen

Melissa had to give Aaron credit. He'd played by her ground rules where her clients were concerned, letting her set up the interviews with the women and not pressing the issue when a couple of her clients declined to talk to either of them. He used extreme discretion in checking up on the men involved, coming up with cover identities that kept the word "sheriff" or "police" out of the conversation.

By Sunday evening, he'd managed to eliminate seven of the eight possible suspects completely, and the eighth suspect wasn't much of a prospect, having lost the use of his legs in a car accident the year before.

"He doesn't look likely," Aaron had conceded. "It would've been hard to get that bomb in the planter on your porch if he's confined to a wheelchair."

"He'd have had to have had an accomplice, and I don't think that's plausible," Melissa agreed, picking up the list and putting an "X" through the last name. "I guess there's some comfort in knowing that I'm not on the top of their most-hated lists after all, huh?"

"They save that for the women in their lives." Aaron leaned back against the sofa, laying his head back until he was staring up at the ceiling. He looked tired and frustrated. She knew he didn't enjoy waiting for Riley and the other deputies to bring him news. He wanted to be on the outside, shaking things up, following leads.

"You're not cut out to be a bodyguard," she said aloud.

He lifted his head, looking at her. "You're not pleased with the service?"

She smiled. "The service is fine." *More than fine,* a treacherous voice in the back of her head added, reminding her of the feel of his firm, hot mouth on hers. "But you'd rather be out there knocking on doors. You're not suited for this self-imposed house arrest."

"I'm happy to be here."

She shook her head, affection blooming like a flower in the center of her chest. "No, you're not."

He sat forward, his eyes narrowing slightly. "Is this your way of telling me you're tired of playing house with me?"

She looked away, wondering what he'd say if she told him the truth—that playing house with him was becoming entirely too delightful for her. She loved having him around. She liked the way he smelled, the sleepy bear look he had early in the morning and the black beard stubble that shadowed his jaw by the end of every day. She liked to watch him when he decided he was in the mood to cook and took over the small kitchen, filling it with his broad, muscular frame and the mouthwatering aroma of the simple, hearty food he liked to prepare.

She even liked the way he sometimes just watched her, his gray eyes perceptive, looking for things inside her that nobody else ever bothered to try to find.

She constantly had to remind herself it was only an illusion. They were playing house, just as he said. It would come to an end, sooner than later. She had to fight against letting herself get too wrapped up in the fantasy.

"I'd like to go into my office today," she said aloud.

"Not a good idea."

"Why? Because you think someone there wants me dead?"

"We haven't completely cleared Dalton Brant."

She shook her head. "Yes, you have. You told me yourself that his alibis all check out."

"He could be working with someone else."

"Who?" She stood up and started to pace, pent up energy making her restless.

"I don't know."

She stopped in the middle of pacing to look at him. "I can't stay here forever. I have a life. A job."

"You have someone who wants you dead."

"Then let him try again!" Frustration burned a hole in her chest. "I'm tired of hiding, Aaron. And what happens when your week's vacation is over? What are you going to do, quit your job?" She didn't miss the pained look in his eyes. "Of course not. If the killer can't come after me here, then maybe I should be out there where he can make his move."

"You've lost your mind." Aaron rose in a burst of pent-up anger, stepping closer to her. "We're still investigating—"

"We're spinning our wheels." She pressed her palm against his chest, feeling his steady pulse against her fingertips. "I want to be normal again. I just—I want to go home."

"Your house won't have electricity until the end of this week, at the soonest," Aaron reminded her. His electrician friend had worked her in as a rush job, but the damage done to her electrical outlet had been pretty extensive. It would take at least until Friday to get all the parts in and get the basic repairs done. Then she might still have a wait if the power company couldn't get there to restore power to the lines.

Aaron covered her hand with his, pressing her palm more firmly against his chest. "Tell you what. We could get out of here for a little while. The weather's supposed to be warmer today. How would you like to go fishing?"

She looked up at him, surprised by the suggestion. "I don't know how to fish."

He smiled. "No problem. I can teach you all you need to know. If you ask nicely, I might even bait your hook for you."

"We're going to use live bait?" She suppressed a shudder.

His eyes narrowed. "This isn't holding much appeal for you, is it?"

"Are there going to be worms involved?"

He grinned. "We can do something else."

"No," she said, tamping down her doubts. "How many chances does a girl have to go fishing with a Cooper for free?"

His smile widened. "Who said it's free?"

MELISSA WATCHED AARON poke through the large metal tackle box at his feet, feeling relaxed for the first time in days. Maybe it was the warm sun beating down on her shoulders, driving away the underlying chill of the day. Or the fresh air filling her lungs with each breath.

Or maybe it was the sight of Aaron Cooper in a pair of snug-fitting jeans and a thin cotton sweater that showed off the broad, muscular chest that had made him the most swoon-worthy guy at Chickasaw County High School.

He picked up the short, lightweight rod he'd selected for her and tied a small chartreuse-colored jig to the end of the nearly invisible line. "Ready to give this a shot?"

"What if I get the line all tangled up?"

"Oh, there's no 'what if' about it. You will." He crossed to where she sat on one of the two fishing seats. He'd given her the more comfortable folding seat, taking the smaller stoollike seat for himself, even though he was clearly too large for it. "But getting tangled up is half the fun," he added with a wicked grin.

She didn't take the bait, even though her temperature notched upwards a couple of degrees. "You Coopers have a strange idea of fun." She took the rod from him. "This is a spinning reel, right?"

"I thought you didn't know anything about fishing."

She wasn't about to explain that all she knew about fishing was what she'd taken care to research all those years ago when she had an outsized crush on him in high school. She had known even then that her chances with Aaron Cooper were slim to none, but she hadn't been the class valedictorian without learning the value of research and preparation.

She poked at the bail, a thin, curved piece of metal that controlled the unspooling line. The winding handle was on the left, unlike most other types of reels. She tried to remember what she'd read about casting with a spinning reel.

"You flip that bail open, which releases the line. Just be sure to keep your finger against the line to hold it in place before you cast." He picked up his own rod, opened the bail and, with an underhand flick, tossed his own bait into the water. He started turning the handle with his left hand and the bait swam back to them. "See how it works?"

Frowning with concentration, she tried to mimic his casual underhand cast. The bail slipped closed and the bait swung up in a violent circle, nearly smacking into her face.

She ducked out of the way, sliding off the seat sideways. Aaron caught her before she tumbled to the deck, his strong arms warm and solid around her waist.

She willed away the furious blush rising in her cheeks. It had looked a lot easier in the fishing books. "Did I mention I'm a total klutz?"

"That speaks for itself," he murmured, his tone light and

teasing. A different kind of warmth flowed up her neck into her face, jump-starting her pulse.

"Maybe I could just watch you fish instead?"

"No ma'am." He gently settled her back on her feet and circled behind her, keeping his arms wrapped around her waist for a moment. He was warm and solid against her back, making her whole body hum with awareness. "Let's give it another try. This time, I want you to try it overhand. Just give a little flick of your wrist and let go of the line at the same time."

He guided her with light touches to her arm and hand. Her fingers trembled, almost making her lose her grip on the rod.

"Rod tip back, then flick forward. Let it go."

She did as he said. The line didn't go out very far, but at least the lure made it into the water."

"That was great!" Aaron gave her shoulders a quick squeeze. "And you're in a pretty good spot, too. See those twigs sticking up out of the water right next to your line? That's the tops of some old Christmas trees we sank to create cover for the fish."

He showed her how to work the jig, whooping with delight when something tugged on her line. She reeled the line in, her movements jerky and fast. The rod bent powerfully, and she fought to keep it from flying from her grasp.

She was certain she was doing everything wrong, but she managed to pull a surprisingly small, plate-shaped fish out of the water and into the boat without any more disasters.

"That's not a crappie, is it?" she asked, surprised by how hard she was breathing.

"Nope, that's a bluegill." Aaron wrapped his huge hand around the fat little fish and held it steady while he removed the hook from its tiny mouth. "And you fought him in like a pro, darlin'. Pound for pound, those fellows give you a better fight than a bass. Just don't tell Jake and Gabe I said that. They're bass purists."

She grinned at him, ridiculously pleased by his praise. "Can I hold him?"

He shifted his hold on the fish. "Easy," he said as she reached for the fish. "His spines are—"

Just as she started to wrap her hand around the small greenish-brown fish, the bluegill spread his dorsal fin, nicking her hand with one of the sharp spines. "Ow!"

"—sharp," Aaron finished too late. He grabbed the fish before she dropped him to the deck. "How bad did he fin you?"

She examined her bleeding palm. "Enough to draw blood."

He dropped the fish back into the lake and took her hand, examining it. "It'll be okay. It might hurt a bit."

It was already stinging. "Do you have a first aid kit?"

"I left it back at the marina, damn it." He frowned, looking annoyed. "I took it to the bait shop for Dad to restock for me a few days ago, and I forgot to get it back from him before we came out."

"It's okay," she said quickly, not wanting to come across as a whiner even though the pricked spot was surprisingly painful. "The bleeding's almost stopped."

"It could still get infected if we don't clean it up. We're not far from the marina. Let's go back to get the kit."

They made it back to the marina in a few minutes, docking at the Cooper family slip, where the family moored their own boats. Aaron led Melissa down the weathered pier to the gravel walkway up to the bait shop.

With the warmer weather, business at the bait shop had picked up, evidenced by the number of vehicles parked in the paved lot beside the shop. Beside Melissa, Aaron's spine straightened and his hands dropped to his sides as if he was preparing for a fight.

She shot him a worried look. "Is something wrong?"

He slanted a quick look her way. "No. Just didn't anticipate a crowd."

"Maybe it's better that way. I would think isolation might be more dangerous." She checked under the handkerchief he'd given her to cover her injured hand. The tiny hole in her palm had stopped bleeding altogether, but the skin around the nick was beginning to swell.

"You're probably a little allergic," Aaron said when she showed him the inflammation. "Once you wash it out, it'll be fine."

Both of Aaron's parents were busy at the front, so he led Melissa to the back room, where a large cricket pen shared space with a couple of large live wells full of minnows, and several rows of plastic bins that seemed to be filled with dirt.

"Worm farms," Aaron said, noticing her curiosity. "Dad raises his own red worms and night crawlers for bait." He searched the shelves closest to the door until he found a small, soft-sided blue pouch with a white cross on the front. "Bingo."

"Raises them?" she asked as he unzipped the bag and started going through the contents.

"Not that hard to do, really." Aaron's brow furrowed. He tried a different side of the first aid kit. "Keep the dirt changed, feed them table scraps. They're low maintenance." He growled with frustration. "I guess Dad didn't get a chance to restock it. Wait here and I'll see if he's got a better kit up front at the counter."

As Aaron hurried out to the front of the store, Melissa moved closer to one of the flat plastic trays. There was a plastic top over the bin with holes in it, no doubt to allow air to circulate inside the tray. The top wasn't snapped closed, so she lifted the edge of the lid and peeked inside.

At first, all she saw was soil, dotted here and there with decomposing pieces of banana peels, potato skins and something brown and desiccated that might have once been an apple core. The smell inside wasn't putrid, as she'd feared; instead, a rich, loamy odor filled her nose, reminiscent of the earthy scent of decaying fall leaves.

Then she noticed that the soil seemed to be vibrating. It took a second to realize that she was seeing dozens, maybe hundreds of red worms wriggling just beneath the top layer of soil.

She dropped the lid back over the tray with a violent shudder, stepping back so quickly that her foot caught on the edge of the shelf behind her, and she fell backward.

"Ow," she groaned as her tailbone connected with the hard concrete floor. She scrambled up before Aaron or anyone else found her sprawled across the bait room floor like the accident-prone idiot she was.

Rubbing her butt, she double-checked the lid on the worm farm to make sure it was safely back in place, then examined her palm to see if the fall had started her wound bleeding again. It looked okay, she saw with relief, though the swelling might be a little worse than before. The earlier sharp pain had settled to a dull ache, however, so she decided not to worry. Aaron would be back soon with the first aid kit. He was a lifelong fisherman. He'd know what to do.

As she wandered to the back of the room, where the large metal minnow tanks sat side by side against the far wall, she heard footsteps behind her. But before she could turn around to greet Aaron, the dim light from the overhead bulbs disappeared, plunging the room into blackness.

It took a second for her eyes to adjust to the darkness

enough to see a thin sliver of light outlining the door that led into the front of the shop.

The door that Aaron had left open when he left.

Her heart skipped a beat, then hit the ground running, hurtling out of control. She backed into a corner and stared into the unrelenting darkness, trying to make out shapes. She'd heard footsteps before, but now there was nothing. Nothing but the hammering cadence of her pulse in her ears.

Suddenly, a voice materialized out of the deep black, closer than she expected. "Hello again, Melissa."

Her head began to spin. She clutched the shelf at her back, fighting to keep her feet as a storm of memories whipped through her, tearing at her soul. Hands on her throat, pressing and squeezing. His unleashed rage ripping into her, as violent and relentless as the pounding of his fists on her flesh. The world seemed to fall out from under her feet, as if she'd fallen off the face of the earth.

"Long time no see," Evan Hallman said in a voice as deep as a nightmare.

"Sorry I haven't gotten around to that yet." Mike Cooper passed change to a customer and turned to look at Aaron. "I was going to do it this morning but the weather turned."

"No problem." Aaron selected a box of antiseptic wipes from the store's first aid section and tossed it into the small plastic shopping basket where antibiotic ointment and flexible bandages already sat. "Although I hate that we had to interrupt the fishing just when she caught her first bluegill."

Mike grinned. "First fish, and already a war wound."

Aaron smiled, remembering the way she'd grinned up at him when she brought the fish into the boat, her cheeks pink from the sun and her eyes reflecting the brilliant blue of the cloudless sky.

He'd never seen anything more beautiful, he thought, a

lump rising in his throat. Not so different from the way she'd looked that night at the first school mixer their freshman year. He'd thought her beautiful then as well.

He just hadn't realized it until now.

What had happened between then and now? How had he let himself become blind to her all those years of high school? He must have had classes with her, passed her in the hall hundreds of times, without even seeing her.

What kind of person had he been?

He shook off his unsettling retrospection and put the basket on the counter. As his father rang up the purchases, Aaron's gaze drifted toward the bait room door, a little surprised Melissa hadn't come looking for him already.

The door was closed.

His spine tingled painfully. He hadn't closed the door, had he? He hadn't thought Melissa would appreciate being closed into the dark, cool room with thousands of creepy-crawlies.

Had she closed the door herself?

He reached behind him on instinct, checking for the Smith & Wesson holstered in the small of his back. He drew the weapon, ignoring his father's look of surprise, and crossed quickly to the closed bait room door.

"Keep everyone clear of this door," he told his father quietly.

Mike nodded.

Aaron tried the knob. The door locked from the outside, so there wasn't any chance that it was locked, but it might be booby-trapped somehow.

It creaked open, louder than he liked. He stayed flattened against the wall, peering quickly around the door frame to scan the interior. The overhead bulbs were dark, so all he saw at first was what daylight from the open doorway revealed—the bait room, still and empty.

"Melissa?"

There was no answer.

He reached inside with one hand and flicked on the light. The half-dozen bare bulbs strung along the ceiling of the cinderblock room illuminated shelves and tanks.

But no Melissa.

His heart in his throat, he moved deeper into the bait room, weapon drawn.

Because of the dirty nature of worm farming, the floor of the bait room was perpetually soiled, swept out only at the end of the day after all the transactions were finished. It was impossible to miss the tangle of footprints that disturbed the grime in front of the minnow tanks.

Or the drag marks leading across the concrete floor to the narrow back door.

Chapter Fourteen

Aaron's heart pounded as he pushed open the back door and looked beyond. The back of the shop butted right up to the woods. Even with many of the trees winter bare, Aaron saw only a wall of knotty tree trunks strangled by underbrush stretching out ahead.

Damn it! How could he have left her alone in that room?

He snapped open his cell phone and called for backup, then dialed Riley directly.

"No chance she wandered off?" Riley asked.

"Drag marks, Riley. Someone has her." Aaron hurried back through the bait room to the front of the shop, catching his father's eye. "I'm heading into the woods after them."

"Wait for backup, Aaron," Riley warned.

Aaron hung up without saying good-bye, turning to his father. "Someone's taken Melissa."

"What?"

"Someone went into the bait room while I was restocking the first aid kit. I'm going after them."

"I'll come with you."

Aaron shook his head. His father's arthritic knees would slow down the pursuit. "You can't, Dad. You know you can't."

"Then I'll see if I can track down your brothers."

Aaron nodded and ran back through the bait shop toward the back door.

Outside, he moved deeper into the woods, scanning the area to get an idea what direction Melissa and her captor might have gone. He'd grown up here, played in these woods his whole life. He knew them like his own skin. They ringed the lake for miles, broken up here and there by lake houses and the occasional narrow dirt or gravel road leading down to piers and boat landings.

The question was, how well did the person who had Melissa know these woods? And could Aaron track them down before it was too late?

SHE HAD FALLEN facedown, her cheek pressed against the hard concrete.

Only it wasn't concrete, was it? Melissa struggled against an enervating sense of hopelessness that weighed her down like a leaden blanket, her senses overwhelmed by smells and dizzying sights that dulled her brain. She wasn't on the sidewalk outside her Durham apartment, every inch of her body aching and broken. She was lying facedown in the woods, her skin clammy against the damp detritus of rotting leaves.

She remembered moving through the woods, tree limbs smacking against her face, leaving scratches.

And fear, as cold as the grave.

She couldn't breathe, couldn't move. Why couldn't she move? She tried to lift her arms, but they were pinned to her sides. Something solid and hot pressed against her back, a stark contrast to the cold softness beneath her prone body.

She heard a swishing sound in her ear. Someone breathing, fast and hard.

Terror rose in an acid bubble in her throat.

Evan. Evan was here. He'd grabbed her at the bait shop,

silenced her with his cruel grip and dragged her out into the woods by the lake. Then, he'd thrown her to the ground, knocking the breath from her lungs. Everything had gone black.

How long had she been out?

"Shh," Evan whispered as she opened her mouth to scream.

She went still, her heart rate galloping out of control. A tiny, terrified part of her wanted to disappear completely, to burrow into the loamy soil beneath her cheek and remain there, hidden and safe.

She buried that shivering little creature deep inside herself, drawing instead on the fierce, determined fighter she'd become in the last four years.

Aaron Cooper was out there somewhere, looking for her. It wouldn't have taken him long to realize she was missing. As long as she stayed alive, he'd find her.

Whatever it took, she had to stay alive.

She twisted her head until she could see Evan out of the corner of her left eye. He was lying on top of her, pressing her down into the forest floor. Was he trying to hide from something? Was Aaron already out there, on the hunt?

"What do you want from me?" she asked.

"Payback, baby." Evan's voice trembled with rage. "You got up there and lied about me to that judge, twisted everything we had into something ugly—"

"You think it wasn't ugly?" She deliberately kept her voice calm, despite the toxic cocktail of fear and fury burning like fire in her belly. "You think it's okay to th-throw a woman off a two-story balcony? For any reason?"

"You wouldn't listen to me!" Evan's voice rose. His grip around her arms and chest tightened painfully. "You never listened to me. You never…did…what I asked—"

Melissa couldn't catch her breath, he was crushing her so tightly to him.

"I've seen you with him. I've watched you for the past few days. I know you're living together."

Blackness started to creep around the edges of Melissa's vision. She tried to make sense of what he was saying. He thought she and Aaron were living together?

"You're mine, Melissa." Evan's arms tightened around her even more. "Understand?"

A buzzing sound rose in her ears, black spots filling her vision. She struggled against unconsciousness, knowing this might be her last chance to make her move.

She couldn't escape his iron grip by struggling. He was too strong. But she could move her head. And Evan's face was right behind hers: she felt the heat of his breath on the nape of her neck.

Pouring every ounce of strength she had into the move, she slammed her head back against his face. Pain blossomed in the back of her head, but it was minor compared to the sound of bones crunching as her skull crushed Evan's nose.

Howling in pain, he loosened his grip. As air flowed back into her lungs, her vision cleared. Adrenaline sizzled through her veins, giving her a surge of strength. She reared up, throwing him off of her, and scrambled to her feet.

Evan's voice rose in a stream of obscenities, but they didn't have power over her any longer. She took a split second to get her bearings. The sunlight dappling the forest floor was still coming from the east, sparkling on the narrow patch of lake water barely visible through the trees. If she headed toward the lake, she'd hit civilization sooner or later.

She set out at a dead run toward the promise of freedom.

AARON WASN'T THE BEST tracker in his family, but he was good enough to follow whoever had taken Melissa out of the bait room into the woods. Broken branches, scattered leaves and scuff marks in the dirt left a clear trail through the underbrush. Within five minutes, he started hearing the sound of crashing through the underbrush ahead. He couldn't see any movement yet but knew he was getting close.

Suddenly, the noise stopped.

Aaron stopped moving, listening. The normal noises of the woods—birds, squirrels, chipmunks—were absent. They were probably watching and waiting for the intruders to leave.

Then he heard a voice ahead. Male. Raised in anger.

Aaron fought to control the surge of adrenaline. He had to be in control.

Suddenly he heard an animal howl of pain, followed by loud rustling, as if someone was struggling in the woods about forty yards ahead. He started moving, as quietly as he could manage, toward the sound, the Smith & Wesson heavy in his hand.

The noises increased. He heard someone running, hard and fast toward the lake, chased by a male voice screaming a stream of ugly invective that made Aaron's blood pressure rise.

Aaron caught a glimpse of the runner, moving with more speed than grace, arms flailing against twigs and branches snagging her pale blue jacket and dark ponytail.

His heart nearly stopped with relief. Melissa.

She was alive.

He dragged his gaze from her, scanning the woods behind her for her assailant. Several seconds passed before he saw a man lumbering behind her, one hand pressed to his nose. Blood streamed from beneath his hand, and Aaron felt a rush of grim satisfaction. She'd wounded the bastard.

That's my girl.

Aaron started moving laterally to intercept Melissa's

pursuer. So focused was the bleeding man on his quarry that he didn't even notice Aaron bearing down on him until it was too late. His dark eyes widened just as Aaron slammed him to the ground at a full run.

Aaron thought he heard ribs cracking. He didn't feel the least bit bad about it.

He used the man's windbreaker as a ligature, trussing his hands to his feet behind him. Blood flowed from the man's crooked, swollen nose as he turned his impotent rage on Aaron.

"Shut up," Aaron ordered firmly, showing his pistol to the bleeding man. "I'm with the Chickasaw County Sheriff's Department. You're under arrest for the abduction of Melissa Draper." He finished reading the man his rights hastily, then called in his position to the Sheriff's Department dispatch.

He could still hear Melissa crashing through the woods toward the lake to his left, but he had to let her go. His prisoner wasn't secured well enough to leave alone.

The sound of movement behind him set his nerves on full alert. He shifted positions, scanning the woods behind him, his Smith & Wesson back in his hand and ready for action.

He spotted someone flitting through the trees, moving in near silence. Dark hair, broad shoulders—Aaron nearly slumped with relief.

It was his brother Gabe.

"He's secure," Aaron called out to Gabe. A moment later, Gabe emerged into the open, moving straight toward him.

Aaron caught him up on what had happened. "You armed?"

Gabe lifted the hem of his jacket to reveal a dark blue Ruger tucked into a waistband holster. He was an auxiliary deputy, usually only called in for manhunts or other situations calling for mass mobilization, but Aaron knew his older brother was good in a fight and well trained enough to handle prisoner containment while he went after Melissa.

"Backup's on the way. I've got to go." He was already running, his gaze fixed on the last place he'd seen Melissa before she disappeared into the trees.

He called her name as loud as he could. "Stop running, it's me!"

He caught sight of her a few seconds later, still running recklessly through the woods toward the water's edge. Ignoring the twinge starting in his left knee where the old injury still gave him trouble now and then, he drove himself faster, cutting half the distance between Melissa and himself within a few seconds.

"Baby, stop running! It's me."

She threw a look over her shoulder at him, her eyes widening as she recognized him. Suddenly, her feet tangled up in the underbrush and she fell headlong into a dense tangle of honeysuckle vines.

Aaron crashed through the underbrush and reached her side as she struggled to find her footing. He plucked her up and pulled her into his arms, his whole body trembling with relief as he felt her heartbeat strong and sure against his chest. She wrapped her arms around his waist, her grip surprisingly strong. Her breath came in ragged gasps against the front of his shirt.

He tangled his fingers in her hair, pulling her face up to look at him. "Are you okay?"

She nodded. "Evan—he's in the woods—"

"He's all trussed up and going nowhere. Gabe's keeping an eye on him until backup arrives." He plucked a dead leaf out of her tangled hair. "Tell me what happened."

Haltingly, she told him about the lights in the bait room going off and, seconds later, Evan's voice in her ear. "He covered my mouth with one hand and dragged me out. I tried to scream, but the door was closed—"

"I'm sorry, I shouldn't have left you there alone." He was sick about what could have happened if he hadn't noticed the door was closed as soon as he did.

"It was—strange—" Her brow wrinkled. "For a few seconds, I felt paralyzed. I wasn't in the woods at all. I was in my apartment back in Durham."

Post-traumatic stress, he thought. Evan Hallman had nearly killed her four years earlier. Maybe she'd had a flashback to that night.

"It was—jumbled." She shook her head. "Then he suddenly threw me to the ground and I think the fall knocked the breath out of me. Everything went black for awhile." She shuddered under his hands. "When I could think again, I was facedown on the ground with Evan lying on my back."

He stroked her face carefully. "Did he—"

Her eyes darkened. "No. I'm not sure he wouldn't have tried if I hadn't gotten away, though. He still thinks I belong to him. After all this time."

Aaron felt a surge of primal rage so strong it was all he could do to stay there with her rather than going back into the woods to kill Evan Hallman.

Melissa's hands lifted to grip his forearms. "Don't leave me," she whispered.

He bent and pressed his lips firmly against her forehead. "Not a chance."

Wrapping his arm around her waist to keep her on her trembling legs, he led her back to the marina.

MELISSA CURLED her hands around the mug of hot chocolate Aaron had coaxed her to drink after dinner, watching him stoke the fire he'd just built in the cottage's fireplace. "You really think Evan was behind everything?"

Aaron returned the iron poker to the stand and came to sit beside her on the sofa. "It's looking likely. We finally got in touch with Hallman's parole officer, and he said nobody in Raleigh's seen Hallman for over a week. That means he could have been here in time to set the fire at your house."

"I wonder why he didn't just break in and come after me." She marveled at how calmly she could discuss the idea so soon after Evan's attack on her that afternoon.

It was because Aaron was here, she knew. Having him next to her, close enough to touch, made her feel like a different person. She felt stronger. Braver.

She'd always thought it would be that way, she remembered. From the first time she'd set eyes on him, she'd felt a powerful connection to him, as if he was the answer to some question she hadn't known how to ask.

"I don't know why he set the fire instead of going inside," Aaron answered. "I'm sure that's going to be one of the questions Riley asks him tonight."

She reached for his hand, closing her fingers around his. "I know you wanted to be there for the interrogation."

He twined his fingers with hers. "I want to be here."

"I want you here, too." She turned to face him, driven by a reckless feeling that had been growing inside her all afternoon. It felt like something alive inside her belly, struggling to emerge, to find freedom and release.

Aaron's eyes darkened as his gaze tangled with hers. "Melissa," he whispered, his breath quickening.

She realized she'd closed the distance between them, her free hand moving up his chest in a slow, deliberate seduction. In a heartbeat, she knew what she wanted.

What she needed.

"Don't," she whispered as he opened his mouth to speak again. She pulled her hand from his and lifted it to his face, cradling his strong jaw between her fingers. She just looked at him for a moment, really looked at him, seeing the boy he'd once been, still trapped in the amber of time, there beneath the masculine lines and planes of his handsome face. "I saw you at the mixer, too," she said, running her thumb slowly over the curve of his bottom lip. "I wanted you to come to me. But I knew you wouldn't."

"I should have," he murmured, his gaze dropping to settle on her mouth.

"Yes," she agreed. "You should have."

His hands slid up her back, hot through the terry-cloth robe. She almost laughed aloud as she pictured what he must be seeing right now, what a sight she must be in her fuzzy, unsexy robe, her face scratched up from her headlong flight through the woods and her hair limp and damp from the shower.

But he didn't seem to see any of that. He didn't let the nubby old robe stop his hands from tracing the contours of her spine, setting her nerves on fire. He didn't close his eyes to shut out the sight of her when he lowered his head and traced the curve of her jaw with his lips.

"I want you," she whispered in his ear, nipping his earlobe between her teeth.

He groaned against her throat. "Melissa."

She silenced him with her mouth, unleashing the passion she'd held in check for as long as she could remember. It didn't scare her anymore, not with Aaron.

She could feel him holding back and growled with frustration, sliding her tongue over his, demanding more.

He caught her face between his hands, dragging her mouth away and gazing up at her, questions shading his eyes.

"I want this," she said, shifting until she straddled his lap. He was hard against her softness, the evidence of her power over him sending fresh determination coursing through her veins. She slid closer, gasping as he surged up against her, another groan escaping his throat.

His fingers fumbled at the sash of her robe, graceless and impatient. Laughing softly, she unfastened the knot for him, amazed at the steadiness of her hands. She knew what she wanted, and for the first time in her life, she was going to throw away all her fear and take what she needed.

And she needed Aaron Cooper. Every part of him, including his self-control.

She'd never needed anything more.

"Don't hold back," she urged, pulling back the edges of her robe to bare herself to his touch.

His eyes burned into hers, feral and fierce. She felt a flush of triumph, unfettered by fear for the first time she could remember.

Then he kissed her and she was lost.

Chapter Fifteen

The bedroom was still dark, though cool gray half-light seeped through the muslin curtains, a harbinger of the coming dawn. Wrapped in Aaron's arms, Melissa didn't want to move, but something had jarred her awake. She listened to the silence broken only by Aaron's slow, steady breathing.

There. Had that been a thump outside the door?

Melissa nudged Aaron. "Wake up. I hear something in the other room."

He didn't stir.

"Aaron!" She kept her voice low as she heard another thump outside the bedroom. They hadn't stopped to close the door last night when he carried her into the bedroom, though now she was beginning to think they should have. What if it was Aaron's mother out there, dropping by early to bring them breakfast?

She couldn't bear the humiliation of being found naked in bed with Aaron by his mother.

She slipped out of Aaron's arms, wincing at the aches and twinges that came with her first effort at movement. Her cheeks grew hot as she thought of the intensity, the abandon with which they'd embraced their desire for each other. Though she hadn't been a virgin, nothing she'd ever experienced had come close to overwhelming her the way making love to Aaron had done.

But had it been a mistake? Her steely control over her desires, her slavish devotion to logic over emotion, had saved her time and again over the past four years as she recovered from the damage Evan Hallman had done to her life.

Had she been crazy to give up her control now to a man who admitted he didn't know if he could ever be a forever kind of guy? Last night, swallowed by desire, she'd told herself she could handle whatever happened in the morning. She was strong enough to walk away without regrets, their night together a wonderful memory but nothing more.

She'd lied to herself. She wasn't that strong.

The sound of movement in the other room dragged her back to a more pressing question. Where the hell was her robe?

In the living room, she remembered with another blush. It had fallen to the floor as their lovemaking intensified, forgotten when Aaron swung her into his arms and carried her into the bedroom.

She opened the closet and found one of her work dresses, a long-sleeved jersey sheath that she paired with a cardigan. Slipping her bare feet into a pair of fleece-lined house shoes, she headed into the living room.

There was no one there.

Puzzled, she looked out the front door. Daylight was barely a pearl-gray promise in the eastern sky. Nobody was up and about yet, not even on the lake where early morning fishermen were a common sight.

She closed the door and locked it behind her, returning to the bedroom. She stopped halfway into the room, staring at the empty bed.

"Aaron?"

"Bitch!" Aaron's voice was just behind her, low and vicious.

She whirled around to face him. He stood in the middle

of the darkened bedroom, enormous and imposing. A flutter of terror took hold in the center of her chest as she caught the maddened light in his smoky eyes.

His hands closed over her shoulders, crushing her flesh. She cried out in pain. "You wanted him. I saw it in your eyes last night. You were wrapped around me, but you were thinking of him, weren't you?" He pushed her backward, until her shoulder blades slammed flat against the wall by the window.

"What are you talking about?" She pushed against his chest, but he didn't budge, caging her against the wall. A fresh rush of fear poured through her body like ice water.

"You're a little whore. You always were." Aaron's voice changed, thickened and hardened.

He sounded like Evan, she realized.

Melissa squeezed her eyes shut as tightly as she could, her mind starting to shut down in self-defense. It wasn't happening. It couldn't be happening.

"You're mine, Melissa." Aaron pushed her into the wall. "Understand?" He shook her, making her teeth rattle. She opened her eyes, terrified by what she'd see.

"Melissa?" Aaron's face was close to hers, his voice suddenly, inexplicably gentle. The hardness of the wall at her back melted into the softness of the mattress where she lay.

She pressed her hand to her chest and felt only her own warm flesh instead of the soft jersey dress she'd been wearing a few moments earlier. And Aaron's hands were gentle, not hard.

But she still couldn't breathe. Terror still gripped her, its tight fist squeezing the breath from her lungs.

She pulled away from Aaron's grasp, rolling off the bed and hurrying to the living room to find her robe. She couldn't find it. She had been certain she'd left it out here. Hadn't she?

Aaron emerged from the bedroom, his expression puzzled.

He'd put on his discarded jeans but left the top button unbuttoned. Melissa found her eyes drawn there, remembering how she'd unfastened that button herself the night before.

She'd been so certain she was doing the right thing.

"Where's my robe?" she asked, her voice tight and raspy.

Not answering, he just stared at her naked body, making her feel exposed and vulnerable. She wrapped her arms around her breasts and turned her back to him.

Behind her, he released a soft gasp. "Oh, God."

She looked over her shoulder at him. He was staring at her back, his expression dark with horror.

"What?" she asked.

He disappeared into the bedroom and came back out, holding her robe. His voice shook when he spoke. "I got up in the night and saw you'd left this in here. I thought you might want it this morning."

She felt foolish for not even having checked in the room for the robe. Just because it was in the living room in her dream—

She gave an involuntary shudder, the images of the dream coming back to her in a vivid rush. "I need to get dressed." She took the robe from him, careful not to touch him as she moved past him down the short hallway and back into the bedroom.

She closed the door behind her, shutting him out, and turned on the light. Curiosity overcoming her, she dropped her robe and looked at her back in the full-length mirror hanging on the bedroom door.

She gasped as well at the sight of the ugly purple bruises splotching her bare back. Surely Aaron hadn't left those bruises on her body last night.

But hadn't she encouraged him to unleash the full measure of his desire? It had been a shattering experience, unleashing her own needs to let them run wild. But her nightmare this morning proved it had been an unsettling experience as well.

Maybe she'd been right before, when she'd told Aaron she might never be ready to trust again. And she certainly couldn't trust a man who only offered a few short nights together with no promise of anything more.

Right now she just needed to get out of here. With Evan in the county jail, almost certainly the person behind the threats on her life, she could leave this place, leave Aaron and his overwhelming personality behind her at least long enough to take a deep breath and remember who she was.

Aaron knocked on the door. "Melissa, we need to talk."

She shook her head, wrapping the robe tightly around her. She tied the sash closed. "I need a shower first." She opened the door and pushed past him, pretending she didn't hear him whisper her name.

She locked herself in the bathroom, breathing hard. Tears burned her eyes and she had to swallow a sob, afraid he might be listening at the door. She'd already bared enough of herself to him in the last few hours.

She'd be damned if she'd let him hear her fall apart.

AARON FELT SICK AT the memory of the purple marks on Melissa's back. He couldn't be sure if he'd left them on her body the night before; she'd been manhandled by Evan Hallman only hours earlier, thrown to the ground and roughed up enough that her clothes had been torn in places.

But he didn't remember seeing bruises on her the night before when he'd kissed almost every inch of her slender body, branding it as his own. Truth was, he didn't remember much at all beyond the fire in his belly and the heat in his blood, matched flame for flame by Melissa's determined seduction.

She'd been a surprise. A revelation. Beneath the fragile kitten beat the heart of a lioness, ferocious and single-minded in her pursuit of pleasure. He'd struggled to keep up with her.

But what if he'd taken things too far? What if he'd destroyed her fragile trust instead?

He heard the bathroom door open. His heart in his throat, he rose from the bed as she entered the bedroom.

She looked surprised to see him. Her face flushed a delicate pink, and her hands instinctively went to the lapels of the robe, tugging them together over her breasts.

His heart sank.

"I'm sorry," he said. The apology seemed inadequate.

She didn't reply, just moved past him into the room and opened the closet. He saw her hand tremble as she touched a long-sleeved sweater dress hanging near the front. She quickly moved past the dress and pulled out a navy sweater. When she finally spoke, she didn't turn around. "Do you really think Evan is behind all that happened to me the past few days?"

Her question caught him by surprise. "I think it's likely. He had a motive and seemed to have the means and opportunity. And attacking you yesterday at the bait shop is pretty damning."

Evan hadn't confessed to anything, asking for a lawyer pretty quickly. But Aaron didn't think the bastard would be able to keep from coming clean about his attacks on Melissa for long. Hallman had taken a hell of a risk coming after her on Aaron's home turf, the reckless act of a man coming unglued.

Melissa nodded slowly, still not looking at him as she laid the sweater on the unmade bed. "You should go to the station today. Maybe you can get him to tell the truth." She turned to the tall chest of drawers by the window and retrieved a pair of jeans. "The shower's free."

Get lost, you mean. He stared at her stiff posture, the "don't touch" aura bristling around her as she kept her eyes averted from him.

He didn't think he could say anything right now to make things better between them. So he didn't try, retreating to take a shower.

The hot water felt good on his aching muscles, and he realized, with a bleak smile, that his night with Melissa had left its marks on his body as well as hers. But he was a strong, tough guy. He could take it.

She was fragile in ways that had nothing to do with her physical size and strength. He should have remembered that fact, remembered that she'd been through a terrible ordeal that had sucked her back into the most devastating, terrifying moment of her life. Seeing Evan again would have been traumatic enough. Having him take her hostage, subject her to the same maddened violence that had almost taken her life—

How could he have taken her seduction at face value? How could he have been so selfish? He knew she wasn't like the other women he'd been with.

He couldn't just walk away from her with no regrets.

He shut off the shower and toweled off vigorously, venting his anger at himself. Dressing quickly, he hurried out to find Melissa, determined this time to tell her how sorry he was for letting his own desires overcome his better judgment.

It probably wouldn't be enough to heal the rift his selfishness had created between them, but he had to try.

He didn't find her in the bedroom or the living room. He was about to check the rest of the house when he heard a knock on the door.

He reversed course, heading for the living room. He

glanced through the fisheye security lens and saw his brother J.D. standing on the stoop.

Aaron opened the door. "What are you doing here so early?"

"Dropped off Melissa's VW. I finished fixing it up last night and thought she might like to have wheels."

Aaron looked past him at the cottage driveway. Only his own truck sat there. "Where is it?"

"Oh, Melissa took it. She said she wanted to run over to Borland to check in at her office. She drove off about ten minutes ago."

"She what?"

J.D.'s brow furrowed. "I thought it must be okay or she wouldn't have gone. You caught the guy who was after her, didn't you?"

"We can't be sure yet." Aaron tamped down his rising anxiety, not entirely sure what scared him the most—the idea that they might be wrong about Hallman being behind the threats on her life—or the idea that she'd just walked out of his life, never to return.

J.D. looked horrified. "Oh, man, I'm sorry. I shouldn't have just handed over the keys—"

"What else could you do—hold her captive until I gave permission?" Aaron motioned for J.D. to follow him inside while he headed for the bedroom to find his cell phone. He dialed Melissa's number and waited for her to answer.

The call went through to her voice mail.

He left a terse message, asking for her to call, then went back to the living room to get his jacket. "I'm going after her," he told J.D. "Can you stay here a little while in case she comes back before I find her?"

"Yeah. Mike's having breakfast with Mom and Dad up at the house. He's already dressed and ready for school, so I'll call, let them know what I'm doing and they'll make sure he gets on the school bus on time." J.D. walked him to the door. "I wouldn't worry too much about her, Aaron. That guy Hallman looks good for the attacks, doesn't he?"

"Yeah," Aaron agreed as he headed out the door. But as he belted himself behind the wheel of the truck, he couldn't shake the feeling that Melissa was in more danger than ever before.

SHE HADN'T made it to the highway into Borland before Melissa regretted her decision to run away from Aaron. With a little time and distance between herself and the nightmare she'd had that morning, she recognized that she'd almost let her delayed reaction to the violent encounter with Evan Hallman erase four years of healing.

She met her own gaze in the rear view mirror, taking a good, hard look at what she saw in her own haunted eyes. *He didn't get anywhere close to killing you this time. You beat him. You saved yourself.*

She'd saved herself the last time, too, hadn't she? She'd fought back, grabbed the railing to break her fall. The doctors had told her that if she hadn't been able to catch herself that way, the fall would have probably killed her. If not for her quick response, despite her horrible injuries, she'd be dead.

Why hadn't she seen the truth before? She'd spent so much of her time in the hospital examining and reexamining her choices from that mixed-up time of her life, terrified that she had become a victim like her mother, that she'd never realized she'd made the right moves in the end.

The minute Evan had crossed over from verbal abuse to physical abuse, she'd ended things. No going back, no giving him a second chance. The second attack, the one that had nearly killed her, hadn't been domestic abuse. It had been attempted murder. Nothing she could have done would have changed a thing.

Why had she let those old doubts, that old shame, drive her away from Aaron when she really wanted nothing more than to go back to the cabin and continue what they'd started the night before? He was scared of forever. So was she. But if she didn't at least try to change their futures, could she live with the regrets?

She was tired of living a life of fear. Tired of making herself feel like a victim when she wasn't.

She eyed the road ahead, looking for a place to turn around. There were no crossroads on this stretch of the mountain road, as the narrow right shoulder led to a sloping drop-off ending in thick woods bordering a steep bluff while the left side hugged the mountain. She finally spotted a pull-off about fifty yards ahead to the right, where a pair of tall steel electrical pylons pierced the sky. She slowed her car to prepare for the turn, suddenly impatient to turn the Volkswagen around and head back home.

Home, she echoed silently, grinning at herself in the rear view mirror.

Her grin faded quickly as she saw a dark green sedan looming behind her, bearing down on her at alarming speed.

Hoping there was room for the speeding car to get around her on the narrow road, she gripped the wheel tightly and edged as close to the right side of the one-lane road as she could. She was getting uncomfortably close to the embankment on the right, but the car flying up behind her should have room to get past her.

As the sedan whipped around her, she turned to glare at the offending driver, who should know better than to drive at such speed on the small one-lane country road. But the sedan's windows were tinted too dark for her to see more than the faint outline of a driver behind the wheel.

Suddenly, the sedan whipped to the right, slamming

sideways into the side of her car, sending her lurching wildly to the right. She fought to keep the smaller car on the road, but the momentum had slid her onto the gravel shoulder. The Volkswagen's wheels couldn't find traction on the loose rocks, and she gasped as the vehicle plunged down the incline toward the looming forest below. She struggled with the steering wheel, which seemed to have a life of its own, ripping out of her grasp.

She sideswiped the trunk of a pine tree, sending the Volkswagen into a spin. It skidded across grass and slammed with a bone-jarring crunch against the slender trunk of a dogwood tree.

The seat belt snapped Melissa into place, but it couldn't keep her head from giving a smart smack against the driver's side window. Pain blossomed in her head, stunning her.

As the pain subsided, she thought she heard her cell phone ringing but she couldn't find her purse. By the time she spotted it lying on the floorboard, the phone had stopped ringing. Rubbing the side of her aching forehead, she unlatched her seat belt and leaned forward to get her purse, wincing as the movement made her head pound. She pulled out her phone and saw that she'd missed a call from Aaron.

She hit redial, twisting her head to look out the window. The sun still wasn't up, though the sky above had a lavender glow, promising dawn was close. She tried to reorient herself, figure out where she was in relation to the road.

Suddenly, Aaron's deep voice was in her ear. "Melissa?" He sounded anxious.

"I've had an accident," she said quickly. "Some idiot going about ninety miles an hour ran me off the road."

"Are you okay?"

"Yeah." She flexed her arms and legs, just to be sure. "Nothing's broken."

"Can you get out?"

"I think so."

"Wait—" Aaron's voice darkened. "Did the driver who ran you off the road stop?"

Melissa peered through the darkness, spotting the embankment to her left. A streak of red clay where the car's hurtling descent had gouged a furrow in the grass. She searched the road above, trying to see if the driver of the other car had even bothered to stop and see if she was okay. She couldn't see the sedan, but she did see someone coming down the embankment toward her, little more than a shadow in the gloom.

Fear began to overtake her initial shock. What if the person who'd hit her had done so on purpose?

What if they were wrong about Evan Hallman? If he hadn't been behind the fire and the shootings and the bombs....

For a brief, terrifying moment, she suddenly imagined that it was Evan coming down the bank toward her, somehow released from jail, set loose to finish what he'd started.

"Aaron—"

She heard a beeping sound. Pulling her phone away from her ear, she saw a "battery low" warning.

Then the phone went off.

"No!" She tightened her grip on the phone, panic starting to set in. She looked back over her shoulder and saw the shadow was even closer.

Think, Melissa. You need to see who it is.

The flashlight. She kept a flashlight in her glove box.

She fumbled with the handle of the glove box, finally getting it open. She groped inside until her fingers closed over the small flashlight stored there. She pulled it out and flicked it on, training it through the window toward the approaching silhouette.

A wonderfully familiar face came into focus in the beam of the light. Her boss, Carter Morgan, was walking toward her, only a few feet away from her now, his expression full of concern.

She lowered the driver's side window, cold air rushing in to bite her cheeks. But she was so relieved to see a friendly face she hardly felt it. "Carter! Thank God—I was afraid—" She cut off, shaking her head. "Can you call the Sheriff's Department for me? My phone battery just died."

Carter stopped beside the car, his gaze still fixed on her face. He just stared for a moment, not answering.

"Carter?" she said, a flicker of unease edging its way through the fog of relief.

What was he doing out here in the middle of nowhere? she wondered suddenly, her heart rate beginning a steady climb upward once more. How did he happen to show up just when she needed his help?

Before she could open her mouth to ask, Carter's hand rose up, clutched around a large, jagged rock the size of a softball. She barely had time to brace herself before he swung the rock straight for her head. She pitched herself sideways, but not quickly enough. The rock smacked against her cheekbone, leaving a trail of fiery pain across the ravaged skin, and her world turned upside down.

Chapter Sixteen

Pain. It throbbed in her face, radiating behind her eye and into her brain, relentless. Melissa tried to reorient herself, sensory overload making her mind sluggish.

She heard a rattling noise and tried to turn her head toward the sound, but something stopped her from moving.

It took another second to realize her body was lodged under the steering wheel of her car. With a twist of her head that sent a bone-jarring flash of pain skating along every nerve ending in her body, she saw Carter Morgan grappling with the driver's door, trying to pull it open.

He couldn't reach her through the window, she realized, because the steering wheel blocked his blows. And he couldn't go around to the passenger door because it was partially folded around the trunk of the dogwood tree that had stopped the car's downward slide.

Unfortunately, that also meant Melissa couldn't get out that way, either.

Still, she forced herself to slide over to the passenger side, farther out of Carter's reach. He reached through the open window, his hand grabbing at her ankle as she scrambled away. She kicked at his hand, landing a solid blow that made him grunt with pain.

"Why are you doing this?" she cried, glaring at him through a red haze of pain.

"Get out of the car, Melissa."

"No."

He stepped back from the window, reached into his jacket pocket and pulled out a small silver gun. "Get out of the car."

She stared down the barrel of the small pistol, shocked. The last thing she'd have ever expected to see Carter Morgan holding was a handgun. Where had he even gotten the thing?

"I will shoot you if you don't get out."

She swallowed hard, finding her voice. "Why?"

For a second, Carter's expression shifted into despair. "It's not that I want to."

"Then don't."

His features hardened again. "Get out of the car, Melissa, or I swear I will shoot you where you sit."

Though his hand shook a little, his voice betrayed steely resolution. If she didn't get out of the car right now, she realized, he would do exactly what he said.

Of course, he'd probably kill her with the rock the second he could reach her but she had a fighting chance against a rock. Sitting in the car, facing down a gun? Even if he was a terrible shot, she was a point-blank target. Nobody could miss such a sure thing.

"Okay," she said, holding up her hands. "I'm coming out. But you have to move away. I'm going to have to go out through the window. The door won't budge."

She eyed Carter warily as he stepped back from the side of the Volkswagen. He still had the gun in his hand, but for now, it hovered somewhere at his side. She breathed a small sigh of relief, knowing even as she did so that the reprieve was temporary.

Carter had come here to kill her, and if she didn't figure

out how to elude him and that gun, she might not be alive when Aaron finally found her.

What had happened to her boss? Carter wasn't just her employer; he was her mentor. He'd handpicked her from dozens of young attorneys fresh out of law school to join his staff. He'd taken her under his wing, made her feel like he valued her both personally and professionally.

What could she have possibly done to provoke him to resort to murder?

"Have you been behind everything that's happened to me?" she asked as she edged closer to the window.

He looked away from her, staring at the ground without answering her question. His skin had a grayish tint, so different from his usual healthy tan.

Soul-sick, she thought, remembering a term that her therapist had used to describe Evan Hallman, when Melissa was trying to make sense of how a man with so much going for him could turn out to be so violent and cruel.

Carter Morgan looked soul-sick.

Was it the affair with Alice Gaines? She could see where lying to his wife and his family could wear on a man, drive him to drink too much or snap at his employees perhaps, but murder?

"Is this about Alice?" she asked softly.

Carter's head snapped up. "Of course it's about Alice. Do you think I'd be doing any of this otherwise?"

"I'm not going to tell anyone about seeing you. I don't get involved in things like that, Carter, you know I don't. I don't like that your wife will be hurt, but I'm not going to tell her. I won't tell anyone."

His expression twisted into a grim half smile. "I guess you haven't listened to the radio this morning."

She stopped moving toward the window, her stomach aching suddenly. "The radio?"

He swung one arm wide. "It's all over the news. The beautiful young woman found murdered in Birmingham."

Melissa stared at him, her mind racing to keep up with what he'd just admitted. A young woman in Birmingham—"Oh, my God. Alice?"

His smile froze on his face like a death mask.

She couldn't wrap her brain around what he'd just admitted. "You killed Alice? That's not possible."

"It wasn't something I planned." He sounded defensive.

She couldn't imagine it was. Carter was a man of words, a man of ideas. The closest he'd ever come to violence was the skeet shooting he'd done in college, garnering him a few of the many awards displayed in his trophy case at work.

Nausea bloomed in the pit of her stomach. She'd forgotten that he was such a good shot. Was he as accomplished with the small silver gun held loosely in his right palm? Probably.

The nausea inched upwards. It wouldn't have been hard for him to hit her car from the woods, either, would it?

"I didn't see you do anything, Carter," she said quietly, remaining in the car. "I couldn't testify to anything."

"You saw us together."

"Having a good-bye dinner before she left on vacation," Melissa said desperately. "I couldn't in all honesty tell anyone that you behaved as anything but her boss. That's all I saw."

His brow furrowed. "You're not stupid. I could see what you suspected."

"Suspicion is not proof."

"Just telling the police you saw me with Alice the night of her death would have been enough to put them on my trail. I can't let that happen. You know what it would do to me. To the firm." Agitated, Carter ran his fingers through his hair. "I can't let anything happen to the firm, Melissa. I'm sorry."

"I love the firm, too. I love my job. I can stay quiet."

His gaze met hers for a moment, and she saw how desperately he wanted to believe her. But that hope left his eyes as if he'd snuffed out a candle. A rattling laugh escaped his throat, and he tightened his grip on the gun, motioning for her to get out of the car. "No, you can't. You're far too honest and honorable. That's why I hired you."

She'd run out of time. Steeling her nerves, she grabbed the roof of the car and pulled herself out of the open window, feet first. No reason to give him a chance to bash her head in while she was trying to get out of the car. She landed on her feet, her eyes immediately scanning the gloom around her for some avenue of escape. But all she saw were woods to one side, the six-foot climb to the road on the other and Carter blocking her path forward.

"Let's get this over with." He sounded sad but resigned.

"Can I ask one more thing?" she stalled, praying Aaron hadn't wasted time trying to get her back on the phone before he came out in search of her. If she could keep Carter talking a little longer, she might have a chance to escape.

He looked at her warily, as if reading her mind. But he finally gave a short nod.

"You must have killed Alice by accident. I know you too well to think you planned it. What happened, Carter?"

Overhead gray clouds had begun to gather, a cold wind whipping around the fallen leaves at their feet. The first few fat drops of icy rain began to fall, glistening in the low light like tears on Carter's angular cheeks.

"She was pregnant," he replied in a voice dark with regret.

AARON EYED the dark clouds gathering in the west, scudding across the sky at a relentless pace, spilling their moisture in sporadic splats against the truck's windshield. The forecast

called for heavy rain by midmorning, which might compli-
cate getting Melissa's car hauled back onto the road.

*Don't kid yourself. Someone ran her off the road. Do you
really think that's a coincidence?*

He tried her cell number again. It went straight to voice
mail. He didn't bother leaving another message.

He couldn't be that far behind her, having left almost as
soon as J.D. told him she was gone. She'd had a ten-minute
head start, tops. He should be near the scene of the crash by
now.

Damn it, why hadn't he read her better that morning? He'd
known she was freaked-out, and given her past, he could
guess why. He shouldn't have retreated to the shower instead
of sitting her down and talking it through. Hell, she probably
thought he didn't care enough to make sure she was okay.
That was his reputation, wasn't it? Love 'em and leave 'em
Cooper?

Ahead, he spotted a dark-colored sedan pulled over on
the side of the road. For a second, he felt a flutter of relief.
That must be where Melissa went off the road. Someone had
probably seen the car down the embankment and stopped to
help. At least that would offer her an extra layer of protection,
in case the accident wasn't quite so accidental.

He planned to pull up behind the helpful passerby's car
and take over from there, but a tingling sensation at the back
of his neck made him change his strategy. About thirty yards
ahead was a turnoff, leading on to a narrow gravel-paved
road. Aaron slowed the truck and took the turn, parking just
off the road. He couldn't see the accident site from here, the
view blocked by trees, which served his purposes.

Because nobody there could see him, either. And he had
a sinking feeling that before this day was over, stealth might
be his best weapon.

"WHAT DID YOU DO when she told you she was pregnant?" Melissa kept her voice low and soothing, knowing her best chance of getting out of this mess alive was to keep Carter from panicking before Aaron got here. She wished she'd remembered to charge up her cell phone. She hadn't had time to warn Aaron that she was in danger before the battery died. He probably figured she'd just been run off the road by a reckless driver.

"I didn't know what to do." Carter sounded confused, as if trying to make sense of all that had happened to him in the past week. "I couldn't—" His voice cracked and he started again. "I couldn't let her tell Laurel about the affair. It would have broken my wife's heart."

She stared at him, trying to keep her expression sympathetic, even though she could barely believe what he was saying. He'd had no trouble cheating on Laurel for God knew how long, but he was willing to kill to keep her from finding out?

Or was that just the lie Carter was telling himself?

"She was going to tell Laurel about the two of you?" Melissa guessed.

Carter's eyes flickered up quickly, as if he'd forgotten she was even there. "She thought the baby would change things, you know? And it would. It would have ruined everything."

Rain was starting to fall, soaking through the cable-knit cardigan Melissa had thrown over her sweater and cotton twill trousers. She had dressed for the office, not for a soaking winter rain. Carter was only marginally better prepared, with a water-resistant trench coat over a chambray shirt and jeans. A dark blue ski cap covered his silver hair completely, but it would soon be soaked through. How long would he stand here in the driving rain, letting her stall him with her questions?

Long enough for Aaron to arrive?

She listened for passing cars, but she'd left the cottage early, before six. The road from the marina was lightly traveled, mostly fishermen headed for a day's fishing. But a cold, rainy morning would keep those numbers down.

"Did you set the fire at my house?"

Carter reluctantly met her gaze. "You saw us together."

"So did a lot of people."

"But you could make the direct connection." Carter's mouth curved in a faint smile. "Who would suspect me, otherwise? Alice and I were very discreet, meeting only in towns where we had no personal connections. Her mother died when she was nineteen. She had no other family."

"Nobody to know she was missing."

"She wanted me to go with her on vacation. I couldn't, of course." Carter's gaze shifted, grew far away as if he were remembering their last night together. "I tried to make her see that she had the wrong idea about us."

"You weren't looking for love."

"I have the only love I need," Carter said firmly. "I thought—Alice was young and modern—you younger people have such a different view of things—"

"You thought she'd be okay with being the woman on the side," Melissa guessed.

"It's how she wanted it, at first." Carter sounded bewildered.

Melissa wondered how such an intelligent man, a relatively worldly man, could be so naive about women.

"Did you set the bombs at my house and Amy DeLong's house?"

His eyes narrowed. "The trip wire was too easy to spot. A residence is not an ideal place for such a thing, but I wasn't sure how to make it motion sensitive without risking the bomb blowing up while I was placing it. I didn't have time to assemble it on the spot—"

Carter's calm assessment of his bomb-making skills sent a chill up Melissa's spine. Did he realize he was talking about killing her—to her face?

At the sound of an approaching car, Carter grabbed her arm, his fingers digging into a bruised spot, making Melissa gasp. He eased his grip slightly, his eyes focusing a moment on her. His expression darkened with sadness. "I'm sorry. I never wanted any of this to happen."

"Then stop it," she pleaded. "Just stop now, before it's too late."

He shook his head. "It's already too late." His expression grew resolute, and the grip on her arm tightened again. "We've got to get away from the road."

He half dragged her away from the narrow strip of cleared land at the bottom of the incline, heading into the thick woods. Within seconds, they were almost out of sight of her car.

Even if Aaron arrived, how would he find her?

She grabbed the top of a bush as Carter dragged her by, snapping the top and leaving it to hang. She hoped Aaron knew something about tracking.

"How are you going to explain this as an accident?" she asked, her breath coming in little gasps more from fear than from the exertion.

"You hit your head in the accident, became disoriented and wandered into the woods, where you fell and fractured your skull."

"Nobody's going to believe that."

"Nobody will be able to prove otherwise." A flicker of pride tinted Carter's voice. "The car is stolen. I left no prints, no hairs. These clothes are pulled from a charity drop-off bin. Any fibers from them will be useless, because I'll have burned and discarded them before anyone can collect the evidence."

He was pleased with himself, she realized. Whatever remorse he might be feeling was tempered with pride that he was smart enough to pull this off without getting caught. She'd told him she knew him too well to think he'd planned Alice's murder. But wasn't that exactly what he'd done where she was concerned? He'd tried to kill her four different times, hiding his tracks each step of the way.

She couldn't reconcile the man before her with the mentor she'd respected and trusted. That Carter Morgan had been everything she admired in a person—smart, educated, refined and gentle.

Maybe she'd only seen what she'd wanted to see, at a time when she needed a dependable, admirable man in her life.

A man who was now determined to kill her.

RAIN SLID under the neck of Aaron's jacket, trickling in icy rivulets down his spine, but he ignored the discomfort and pressed on, following the trail of broken branches through the thickening woods. He'd found Melissa's car, with the dead cell phone still lying on the seat but no sign of her or the occupant of the damaged car parked at the side of the road above. He'd gotten the license plate number and phoned it in, but he hadn't had time to wait.

Putting his phone to vibrate, he had started searching the area until he came across an obvious trail.

The soft roar of rain on the tree canopy masked any noise ahead, but Aaron knew he was getting closer to wherever Melissa had gone.

He could feel her.

It was crazy, wasn't it, feeling so connected to her that he knew, on instinct, she was still alive somewhere close ahead? But he knew it was true, just as he'd known, that moment he'd looked across a crowded gymnasium and spotted the shy girl with the long, dark hair and the simple blue dress dancing to her own music, that she would one day change his life.

It had just taken over a decade to happen.

His phone vibrated against his side. He reached into his jacket pocket and pulled it out, peering at the display through the gloom. Riley's number.

"Where are you?" Riley asked without preamble.

Aaron kept his voice low. "Off Three Mile Road around mile marker two. I'm tracking her and the unknown assailant west toward the bluff. Anything yet on the plates I called in?"

"We got a call out of Pea Creek—the car was stolen from someone's backyard sometime overnight."

Aaron pushed back against a sudden surge of fear. Whoever had taken Melissa probably left his own vehicle within walking distance. "Put some officers in that area. Have them search a ten-mile perimeter around the victim's house."

"You think he left his own car nearby."

"Yes."

"Any sign of Melissa and the assailant?"

"I'm tracking them. I don't think they're too far ahead."

"I've sent backup. They should be there in minutes."

"Tell them to hold back on the road. I don't want anything spooking this guy any more than he already is."

"There's something else that's happened—I think it's connected. The morning newspaper had an article about a body found in Birmingham—I guess it made it to the paper up here because the victim lives in the county. Her name is Alice Gaines."

It took a second for Aaron's memory to click in. "The clerk from Melissa's office."

"Hannah told me she was talking to Melissa the other day about office politics—you know, wondering if there was a connection to what was happening to Melissa now. And Melissa mentioned she'd seen two of her coworkers together in Birmingham last week. Coworkers not married to each other. But she refused to name them."

Of course. Melissa would never gossip about a coworker. She'd probably have been reluctant to bring up the subject at all, if not for the rising threat against her.

"If she saw Alice with the man in Birmingham, then what she saw might make our mystery man the prime suspect in Alice Gaines's murder. I'd say that's a pretty powerful motive to try to kill Melissa."

Son of a bitch.

Movement ahead in the woods caught his eye. He crouched, lowering his profile.

"Aaron?" Riley asked.

"Gotta go." Aaron shut off the phone completely and put it back in his pocket, his gaze fixed ahead. The rain had settled into a steady downpour, keeping dawn at bay. Remaining statue-still, Aaron waited for whatever had moved before to disturb the deep green gloom ahead. Finally, a flicker of pale blue flashed in the murk, thirty yards away. Aaron heard the faint rumble of a male voice, muted by the driving rain.

He picked a path through the underbrush and set off, barely able to constrain the urge to get up and run toward the movement ahead. He compromised by quickening his pace, the rain masking any extra noise he might make by moving with less care.

His quarry wasn't taking any precautions, hurtling through the woods in a noisy rush, crashing through the underbrush, voices audible even over the relentless beat of the rain.

Aaron's heart stuttered a moment as Melissa's voice rose over the watery roar. "Nobody's going to believe I wandered this far with a head injury."

Aaron reached the edge of the trees where they thinned

out near the rim of a tall bluff. He finally got a clear look at Melissa, who was drenched to the bone, her cheek oozing blood that ran in rivulets down the side of her face to stain the collar of her pale green blouse. She was struggling with a man dressed in a dark ski cap, jeans and a dark gray slicker. His arms ensnared her as she fought to get away.

"They'll believe you got disoriented by that knock to your head and wandered off the bluff," the man answered in a deep, resolute voice. "And even if they don't, they won't connect me to what happened to you, will they?"

The man spoke in a cultured tone, with only a faint southern accent. He must be the man Melissa told Hannah about, the man having the affair with Alice Gaines. Aaron had gotten a list of Melissa's coworkers around the same time he'd taken Dalton Brant in for questioning, he remembered, straining to put a name to the face of the man in front of him. Melissa's assailant was in his fifties, at a glance, which eliminated everyone but the top man, Carter Morgan and his partner, Charles Dailey.

Carter was the boss Melissa had mentioned, he remembered. Dailey was in charge of the criminal division of the firm, while Morgan ran the corporate law side. She'd have more to do with Carter, he decided. He took a chance as the man dragged Melissa closer to the edge of the bluff. "Carter Morgan, let her go!"

The man froze, peering into the woods behind them.

Melissa increased her struggle, nearly pulling free of the man's grasp. But he grabbed her up against him, staggering backward several steps.

Aaron's breath caught as he realized the man didn't know how close he was to the bluff. "Don't go back!"

But he was too late. Softened by the rain, the edge of the bluff gave way under the man's weight, and he and Melissa plunged out of sight.

Chapter Seventeen

It was happening again.

It hadn't been raining the night that Evan had broken into her apartment. The night had been mild for late April, the handhold beneath her aching fingers cool metal instead of rough, water soaked wood.

But here she was again, holding on for dear life, with almost-certain death lying several feet below.

When the earth gave way beneath her shoes, she'd grabbed for any handhold she could find, her fingers catching and clinging to a tree root jutting from the face of the bluff in a gnarled loop. She'd wrenched her arms in doing so, but so far the root had held, keeping her from sliding farther down the steep slope to the rocks below.

She didn't dare look down to see what had happened to Carter. If she looked down, she'd be lost.

She'd heard Aaron's voice, hadn't she? He'd called out Carter's name, just before they'd gone over the edge. She was almost afraid to call out for him, afraid he wouldn't answer. That he was a figment of her desperate imagination.

"Melissa!" She heard his voice over the rising wind, the sound rippling through her like a burst of energy.

"I'm here!" she called, her voice raspy and weaker than she hoped. She blinked away the blurry film left by the falling rain and peered up at the edge of the bluff about four feet above her.

Suddenly she felt something grab her ankle, adding weight to the strain she was already putting on her arms. She kicked her legs on instinct, but the movement almost made her lose her grip on the tree root. Pressing herself against the muddy side of the bluff, she dared a quick look down.

Straight into the black hole of Carter Morgan's pistol barrel.

He was balanced on a rocky outcropping below her, one hand still tight around her leg. She barely recognized the handsome face now twisted with anger, streaked with blood and red clay from the fall.

With Evan the danger had been from above, from his taunts and the bone-crushing blows of the candlestick against her aching fingers. With Carter the danger lay below, threatening to drag her down to the large, jagged rock bed at the bottom of the bluff.

From above, crumbling chunks of soil rained down on her. She looked up desperately and saw Aaron flattened on his belly at the edge of the cliff, his head and arms jutting over the side. His gaze slid past hers to lock on Carter's gun.

Melissa forced herself to risk another dizzying look beneath her, where Carter stared up at her with pure desperation. "Don't shoot him," she pleaded, her voice a panicked croak.

With a grim smile, Carter aimed his gun at the edge of the bluff and pulled the trigger.

The noise was louder than she expected, making her whole body jerk. She cried out as her grip on the tree root loosened, threatening to let go altogether. The hand on her ankle gave a hard tug, catching onto her tennis shoe. As the laces stretched to the breaking point, the shoe slid from her foot, falling below with a distant thud.

Carter stared up at her, his eyes wide with fear. She felt his fingers slide down her foot, grasping, straining for something to hold until he finally lost his grip on her leg. Time seemed to freeze into an endless loop as he fought to stay upright, teetering on the narrow outcropping beneath his feet, but the kick-back from the gun had been too strong. He toppled backward, his arms flailing, fighting against gravity.

Melissa pressed her face against the side of the bluff, her eyes shut, until she heard the impact on the rocks below. Then there was nothing but the sound of her breathing and the unending patter of rain against her cheeks.

She forced herself to look up, terrified by what she might see. Had Carter's final shot hit its mark? Was Aaron lying dead on the top of the bluff above her?

Aaron peered down at her, his eyes open and bright with life. Her entire body buzzed with relief, threatening to weaken her life-sustaining grip even further.

"Get me up from here," she begged him. "Please!"

He pushed his body a little farther forward, moving carefully as the bluff threatened to give way even more, and reached his long arm down to her. "You're going to have to let go with one hand," he called.

No. She couldn't let go. If she let go, she'd die.

"Please, baby. Please trust me. If you let go, I'll catch you. I promise."

Trust. It had been so long since she had really trusted anyone, she wasn't sure she knew how to do it anymore.

"I'll never let you go," Aaron said, his voice firm and full of promise.

She grounded herself in the solid strength of his gaze. Taking a deep breath, she let go with one hand and dug her feet into the side of the bluff, pushing upward, her free hand outstretched.

Their fingers touched. Tangled. Finally gripped. Aaron's fingers crushed hers, but pain had never felt so good. He coaxed her to let go with her free hand, shouting encouragement when for a brief second the world seemed to disappear from beneath her feet as she dangled in his grasp.

Then, before she could catch her breath again, she was wrapped in his big, powerful arms at the top of the bluff.

AARON SAT beside Melissa's hospital bed, his hands closed over hers, watching her sleep. The doctor had reassured him that she didn't seem to have a concussion, despite the nasty bump on the side of her head, and that they were only keeping her here overnight to be sure she didn't suffer any ill effects from her mild case of hypothermia.

She'd assured him she was fine before the ambulance came to take her away, and later she'd assured him, sleepily, that she was still fine when she was finally put in a private room and the doctors allowed him to visit.

She'd been asleep for almost an hour, her breathing slow and steady. He knew. He'd counted every breath.

The door to the hospital room opened. Riley and Hannah entered quietly, glancing at Melissa before settling their gazes on Aaron's tired face. "How's she doing?" Hannah asked.

"She's going to be okay," he answered, although he might feel a little more sanguine about his answer if she'd wake up and talk to him again.

"Just thought you'd want to know we just put Evan Hallman in a Raleigh police car. He's headed back north to finish out his sentence since he violated parole."

That would buy Melissa a few more years of peace, Aaron thought. "Are we sure Carter Morgan was behind all the other attempts on Melissa's life?" He knew what Melissa had told him about Carter's confessions, but he'd thought putting Hallman in jail had ended the threats to her before. He couldn't afford to be burned again. Not with Melissa's life at stake.

"We executed a search warrant about two hours ago and found equipment we've connected to the pipe bomb and the fire. We haven't found the rifle that shot out her tire yet, but Morgan was a competitive shooter, so he had the means to pull it off."

Hannah put her hand on Aaron's shoulder. "Have you eaten anything today?"

He looked up at her, surprised by the question. "No."

"Why don't we go get you something from the cafeteria?" She tugged at Riley's arm.

He looked a little surprised to be dragged away, but the look in Hannah's eyes brooked no argument. Aaron watched them beat a hasty retreat, bemused, until he turned his gaze back to the bed and saw what Hannah must have seen.

Melissa was awake.

"You're still here," she murmured, sounding surprised.

Before Aaron could answer, there was a soft tap on the hospital door. It opened to reveal Karen Draper's pale, worried face.

She caught sight of her daughter in the bed. Her face whitened even more. "Oh, baby."

Aaron stepped back as Mrs. Draper rushed in. Behind her Derek Draper hovered in the doorway, clearly uncertain whether he was welcome inside. He met Aaron's gaze, his eyes dark with equal parts worry and guilt.

"Your father's here," Aaron told Melissa, who was wrapped in her mother's embrace and murmuring words of reassurance.

Melissa followed his gaze to the doorway. "Come in, Dad."

Draper walked slowly to the bed, his face blanching with each step. Remembering what the man had told him about his vigil at Melissa's bedside four years earlier, Aaron could imagine what was going through Draper's mind.

Draper held his hand out toward his daughter. Aaron found himself holding his breath.

Melissa met Aaron's gaze first, her eyes blazing with a jumble of emotions. He saw fear there, but also relief and hope. As he studied her face, color rose in her cheeks, and her blue eyes grew warm and strong. She reached out and took her father's hand, giving it a light squeeze before letting go.

It was a start.

While her mother fussed over her, Draper stayed in the background, seemingly content to watch her from that distance. Aaron headed outside to waylay Hannah and Riley, knowing Melissa needed a little uninterrupted time with her parents.

Hannah saw him first, her eyebrows arching. "She kicked you out?"

"Her parents are in there."

"Oh. Well, here." She took the two plastic-wrapped boxes Riley held and handed them to Aaron. "We've got to run take Cody off Mama's hands."

They disappeared down the hall.

Aaron walked to the end of the hospital corridor, where a couple of benches lined the windows creating a makeshift waiting area from which he could still see Melissa's room.

He had so much to say to her. Things he didn't want to say in front of an audience. But he knew she needed time with her parents. And they needed time with her. He could wait.

If all went as he hoped, they'd have a whole lifetime together to figure out the rest of it.

"YOU'RE REALLY OKAY?" Karen played with the loose strands of hair falling over Melissa's forehead, making her skin tickle.

Melissa caught her mother's hand firmly in her own. "I'm fine."

"Nobody would tell us anything except that you were being rushed to the hospital." Her father's soft words were the first she'd heard from him since he'd entered the hospital room.

"I'm sorry. I should have called you."

"Don't." Her father's voice sounded strangled. "Don't ever apologize to me. Not after what I put you and your mother through."

The emotion in his eyes shocked her to the core. Anger, she was used to. Contempt and bitterness she'd seen a thousand times. But never regret. Never earnest sorrow.

Her mother had told her she needed to forgive her father, and she supposed that was true. But was she ready?

Not yet.

But for the first time in years, she thought forgiveness might be possible one day.

She saw the shift in her father's expression, as if he saw the softening in her eyes. It wasn't much to offer him, but he looked grateful anyway.

Still, it was a relief when her father cupped her mother's elbow and quietly suggested they should let her get some rest. She watched them go, tugged in opposite directions by her conflicting emotions.

Small steps, she reminded herself.

A few seconds after her parents left, Aaron appeared in the

doorway. Her heart frolicked against her ribs a few seconds, stealing her breath. She pressed her hand to her chest.

"Still awake?" he asked, entering the room.

"Still here?" she countered.

He sat on the edge of her bed, close enough that her heart rate continued dancing around. "What did you think, I'd ditch you the first chance I got?"

She smiled. "It's happened to me before."

He kissed the soft pads of her fingers. Tingles scampered up her arm. "Never again," he promised.

Her smile faded. "I thought you didn't use words like never and ever."

He cradled her hand between his palms against his chest. "Yeah, we need to talk about that."

"I need to say something first." She gathered up her courage, finding it remarkably easy to be daring now that she'd stared death in the face again and won. Compared to dangling from the side of the bluff, telling Aaron Cooper the truth about her feelings was—well, it was equally hard, she had to admit. But she'd lived through the fall. She could live through whatever the next few minutes brought.

What she couldn't live with was letting Aaron walk out of her life without at least trying to change his mind.

"I don't regret last night," she said quietly. "Not a second. I know I probably made you think otherwise—"

He looked surprised. "You ran away."

"I freaked out." She closed her fingers around his. "I know you don't think relationships last. I don't have evidence to argue otherwise. But I can't throw away a chance to be with you just because I'm afraid of getting hurt again."

Aaron turned his palm toward hers, their hands flattening together. He had a strange, shell-shocked look. "I thought it would be a lot harder."

"What would be harder?"

"Deciding we belong together." The certainty in his voice was the last thing she'd expected.

He was right. It was easy. Too easy. She didn't trust things that came too easily. "So you decided. Just like that?"

"I went to take a shower and you disappeared from my life," he answered simply, his voice rich with feeling. "I didn't know if you'd ever come back. And the very thought of never seeing you again was the worst thing that ever happened to me."

She stared at him. It was exactly how she'd felt, hanging from the tree root on the rainy bluff that morning, in the second before she'd dared to look above her to see if Carter's shot had hit its mark. The mere thought that Aaron might have been killed, that she might never see his crooked smile or the teasing light in his eyes again—

"I had a feeling, that moment in the gym all those years ago at the mixer, that you would change my life." He bent toward her until their foreheads met. "And you did."

She caught his face between her palms, gently moving him away so that she could look into his beautiful eyes. He kissed her lightly on her lips, the touch a little tentative, as if he was afraid of demanding too much too soon. But she wrapped her arms around his neck, pulling him down to her in a fierce, demanding embrace, and lost all sense of time and place for several long, breathless moments.

She finally nudged him away from her, laughing softly as he almost fell off the bed trying to regain his equilibrium. "I know we have a lot to talk about, but my meds are starting to kick in again. I just need to tell you—" She struggled against the drowsiness making her eyelids droop. "I need to tell you—I think I might love you." The final words came out in a whisper as her eyelids fluttered shut.

Aaron smiled as her face softened with sleep. Bending over her, he pressed his lips against her forehead briefly, then laid his cheek to hers. "I think I might love you, too," he whispered, his heart so full he thought it might burst.

Still holding on to her hand, he settled back into the chair to watch her sleep.

* * * * *

Don't miss more COOPER JUSTICE *stories from Paula Graves, coming in 2011 and available wherever Harlequin Intrigue books are sold!*

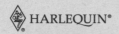
HARLEQUIN®

INTRIGUE®

COMING NEXT MONTH

Available October 12, 2010

#1233 CHRISTMAS COUNTDOWN
Bodyguard of the Month
Jan Hambright

#1234 BOOTS AND BULLETS
Whitehorse, Montana: Winchester Ranch Reloaded
B.J. Daniels

#1235 THE SPY WHO SAVED CHRISTMAS
Dana Marton

#1236 SILENT NIGHT STAKEOUT
Kerry Connor

#1237 DOUBLE-EDGED DETECTIVE
The Delancey Dynasty
Mallory Kane

#1238 A COP IN HER STOCKING
Ann Voss Peterson

LARGER-PRINT BOOKS!

GET 2 FREE LARGER-PRINT NOVELS

PLUS 2 FREE GIFTS!

HARLEQUIN®

INTRIGUE®

Breathtaking Romantic Suspense

HARLEQUIN®

A Romance

FOR EVERY MOOD™

Spotlight on

Inspirational

Wholesome romances
that touch the heart and soul.

See the next page
to enjoy a sneak peek from
the Love Inspired® inspirational series.

*See below for a sneak peek at
our inspirational line, Love Inspired®.
Introducing HIS HOLIDAY BRIDE
by bestselling author Jillian Hart*

Autumn Granger gave her horse rein to slide toward the town's new sheriff.

"Hey, there." The man in a brand-new Stetson, black T-shirt, jeans and riding boots held up a hand in greeting. He stepped away from his four-wheel drive with "Sheriff" in black on the doors and waded through the grasses. "I'm new around here."

"I'm Autumn Granger."

"Nice to meet you, Miss Granger. I'm Ford Sherman, from Chicago." He knuckled back his hat, revealing the most handsome face she'd ever seen. Big blue eyes contrasted with his sun-tanned complexion.

"I'm guessing you haven't seen much open land. Out here, you've got to keep an eye on cows or they're going to tear your vehicle apart."

"What?" He whipped around. Sure enough, mammoth black-and-white creatures had started to gnaw on his four-wheel drive. They clustered like a mob, mouths and tongues and teeth bent on destruction. One cow tried to pry the wiper off the windshield, another chewed on the side mirror. Several leaned through the open window, licking the seats.

"Move along, little dogie." He didn't know the first thing about cattle.

The entire herd swiveled their heads to study him curiously. Not a single hoof shifted. The animals soon returned to chewing, licking, digging through his possessions.

Autumn laughed, a warm and wonderful sound. "Thanks,

I needed that." She then pulled a bag from behind her saddle and waved it at the cows. "Look what I have, guys. Cookies."

Cows swung in her direction, and dozens of liquid brown eyes brightened with cookie hopes. As she circled the car, the cattle bounded after her. The earth shook with the force of their powerful hooves.

"Next time, you're on your own, city boy." She tipped her hat. The cowgirl stayed on his mind, the sweetest thing he had ever seen.

Will Ford be able to stick it out in the country
to find out more about Autumn?
Find out in HIS HOLIDAY BRIDE
by bestselling author Jillian Hart,
available in October 2010
only from Love Inspired®.